M A

FOLK
TALES

MAYO

FOLK TALES

TONY LOCKE

ILLUSTRATED BY GAYNOR LOCKE

The
History
Press
Ireland

This book is dedicated to my wife and soulmate,
Gaynor, with love and appreciation
for all her support over the years.

First published 2014, reprinted 2016

The History Press Ireland
50 City Quay
Dublin 2
Ireland
www.thehistorypress.ie

The History Press Ireland is a member of Publishing Ireland,
the Irish book publishers' association.

© Tony Locke, 2014
Illustrations © Gaynor Locke, 2014

British Library Cataloguing in Publication Data.
A catalogue record for this book is available from the British Library.

ISBN 978 1 84588 847 3

Typesetting and origination by The History Press
Printed and bound by CPI Group (UK) Ltd, Croydon, CR0 4YY

CONTENTS

ACKNOWLEDGEMENTS

This book would not have been possible without the support and encouragement of my wife, Gaynor. Words cannot express my gratitude for her advice and guidance and the amount of time she spent proofreading. Her superb illustrations are a joy to the eye.

My thanks to our daughter Siobhán for her patience, understanding and endless cups of tea.

I would also like to thank Tony Cranston, a fellow storyteller, for his advice, experience and comments, as well as Turtle Bunberry ('The Night of the Big Wind'), Gerard Delaney and the *South Mayo Family Research Journal* ('The Night of the Big Wind'), Ivor Hamrock, Mayo County Library, Jack O'Reilly and his daughter Gertrude O'Reilly McHale.

Finally, I'd like to acknowledge all those storytellers past and present, for a story does not become a story until it is shared and in the sharing it makes the journey a lot shorter.

INTRODUCTION

Those magic words 'once upon a time' have been spoken around the flickering flame of the turf fire by storytellers for thousands of years. In these pages you will find gathered together tales of County Mayo to ignite your imagination: tales of highwaymen and ghostly figures that roam the woods, monsters that inhabit the deep waters of Lough Mask and creatures of the night that suck the life from those they visit.

The stories are part of the rich tapestry that makes up the folklore, myth and legend of Count Mayo and they will take you on a journey through the rugged landscape of the west coast of Ireland, to its holy mountain Croagh Patrick, known locally as 'the Reek', and across the waters of Clew Bay. You will read of Gráinne Ní Mháille, the Pirate Queen, the spectre known as the *Fear Gorta* that roamed the famine villages of west Mayo, and the matchstick man of Straide.

Within the covers of this book, you will also find the story of 'The Love Flower' with its two young lovers, the land of eternal youth known as Tír na nÓg, 'The Night of the Big Wind' and many more. So why not pull up a chair and sit awhile? You know you're never too old for a story.

THE LEGENDS OF BARNALYRA WOOD

Barnalyra was mentioned in O'Donovan's Ordnance Survey (1838), where it was recorded as being the property of Lord Dillon. It covered 796 acres of hilly ground and the soil was described as gravelly, suitable for growing oats and potatoes. There was a deep, wooded ravine on the land, which runs parallel to the road, although most of the trees have since been felled. This was known as Barnalyra Wood and it was located just next to where Knock International Airport is today. The wood is long gone and the few remaining stumps and trees resemble tombstones in a deserted graveyard. This quiet and desolate spot seems to invite you to imagine all sorts of ghostly apparitions and what follows is a tale of one such ghost.

THE GHOST OF BARNALYRA WOOD

The Irish Tourist Association Survey of 1944 records the fact that, in the parish of Kilbeagh in County Mayo, not far from Charlestown, there is a local legend that speaks of greed, heartbreak and a curse that was to lead to the haunting of Barnalyra Wood.

Once there was a poor woodcutter and his wife who lived in a small simple cottage on the edge of the wood. They had one child, a son; however for economic reasons he had gone to England to make his fortune. The cottage was next to the road that led from Sligo to Galway, so a number of travellers would pass by their door each day. One summer's morning there was a knock on the door, which came as a surprise as no coach had stopped. The woodcutter opened the door to find a passing traveller who informed him and his wife that he had word from their son, saying that he was returning from England. In great excitement, the woodcutter and his wife began to make preparations for their son's return.

The son arrived in due course with a travelling companion. They were very tired as they had walked from the town of Drogheda but great joy was felt in their little cottage that night. The son and his friend were given a hearty meal and afterwards they all sat around the blazing fire, smoking their pipes and talking about times gone by and all the strange things they had seen in England. However, the conversation soon turned to the subject of money and how much they had made while working across the water. Of course, the woodcutter found all this boasting a little hard to believe as he didn't think anyone could make that amount of money, so the son's companion took out a large purse filled with gold coins as proof of his earnings. Unfortunately for him, from that moment on his fate was sealed.

As the evening wore on, the son and his friend began to suffer the effects of their long day and decided that they would retire for the night. However, as it was such a small cottage, there were only two bedrooms: one for the woodcutter and his wife and the other for the son. The son and his friend had no option but to share the bed, the son on the inside and his friend on the outside. The woodcutter wished them a good night, closed the door and went back to his wife by the kitchen fire. The son went straight to sleep but his friend found sleep hard to come by and lay awake listening to the sound of voices coming from the kitchen. The woodcutter and his wife were arguing and although he didn't like to listen he found himself drawn to the sound. Imagine his horror when he discovered the reason why they were arguing.

The woodcutter was planning to kill him and take his purse of gold. The wife insisted that this was wrong and that no good would come of it but the woodcutter was adamant and would not be dissuaded. The stranger heard the soft sound of footsteps approaching as the woodcutter, armed with a hatchet, crept stealthily towards the room. The stranger crawled over his friend and lay down on the inside of the bed, hoping that the woodcutter would not be able to attack him without waking his son. Unfortunately, it was a dark night lit only by a faint moonbeam coming through the window, so the woodcutter mistook his son for the stranger and brought the hatchet down on his neck, killing his only son. In the confusion that followed, the stranger escaped, never to be seen again.

About a week passed and the woodsman began to hear a rumour about a headless ghost haunting the road leading from the wood. At first people laughed at the rumour, putting it down to superstition and imagination. However, it wasn't long before more and more people began to report sightings and it was said that even though it was headless they could hear an unearthly screaming coming from the ghost. The rumour soon spread and travellers began to stay clear of the area. It is said that the ghost of their son may still be seen in Barnalyra Wood. Sometimes the ghostly apparition is seen without its head, crying in a sad, unearthly way as he 'curses his father but blesses his mother'.

We don't really know what happened to his parents. Were they convicted of the crime of murder? Did they bury the body and get away with it? I guess we'll never know; however, some people claim they were driven mad by grief and suffered their own death a thousand times before eventually shuffling off this mortal coil. As for the ghost, well, if you're walking near Barnalyra Wood in the dark of night and you hear a faint scream, walk a little faster.

The Irish Highwaymen

The Irish highwaymen were at the height of their powers around the seventeenth and into the late eighteenth century and were particularly active on the main roads leading to and from cities in Kerry, Cork, Dublin and Galway. They had a romantic air about them, a little bit like the Irish version of those famous English outlaws, Robin Hood and Dick Turpin. It was said that, like their English counterparts, they only robbed the rich (usually English or Anglo-Irish landlords) and left the poor peasants alone. For this reason they were generally aided by the peasants who offered them aid and shelter or a place to stable their horse.

However, this in itself carried a severe risk for if you were caught harbouring a highwayman the penalty was death by hanging. It was even said that you would be denied a decent burial in consecrated ground; instead you would be buried at the crossroads or in the local *cillín*.

The term 'rapparee' comes from an Old Irish word meaning a pike-wielding person. The pike was a long thrusting spear used in close combat. Rapparees were usually footpads (common robbers). The footpads had no scruples; they formed small gangs and would just as soon rob the priest of his collection money as thrust a pike into an English gentleman for the gold in his purse.

The highwaymen, however, were a higher class of criminal. It was said they were Irish gentlemen who had been robbed of their land by the English invaders during Cromwell's infamous time in Ireland. These dispossessed Irish gentlemen usually had some military training, could afford a horse, a gun and sometimes a short sword rather than a pike, and they usually didn't murder their victims.

There are many stories told concerning the exploits of the highwaymen, some in song, including 'The Wild Rover', 'Brennan on

the Moor' and, one of my favourites, 'Whiskey in the Jar', a song of betrayal which is said to refer to Patrick Fleming who was hanged in 1650.

In County Mayo we had our own notorious highwaymen, two of whom were known to use Barnalyra Wood as a hideout, although at different points in history. Their names were Dudley Costello and Captain Gallagher.

Dudley Costello

Every county in Ireland had their own 'gentlemen of the road', also known as highwaymen or thieving blackguards, depending on which end of the weapon you were on. County Mayo was no exception. Dudley Costello was known as 'the scourge of Mayo' and Barnalyra Wood was his favourite hideout. The Costellos were descended from an early Anglo-Norman family that had settled in County Mayo. As with many of the Normans who arrived here, they went on to intermarry with indigenous Irish families and soon adopted native ways, becoming 'more Irish than the Irish themselves'. However, it was for this reason that they incurred the wrath of the English authorities in Ireland and after the unsuccessful Irish rebellion of 1641 their lands were seized and given to what the English saw as loyal Crown subjects.

The Costello lands were given to the Dillons. In 1660 Dudley Costello, who had witnessed the distribution of his estates, decided enough was enough. His answer came in open revolt against the English and all they stood for. He gathered a couple of dozen followers who were veterans of various conflicts, including the 1641 rebellion. As veterans, they were trained in the use of sidearms. They took to the woods and hills of County Mayo and they were soon attacking the new planters. Costello became so successful that the State papers of the time described him as the 'Scourge of Mayo'. They began to go further afield, from Lough Mask in County Mayo to Lough Erne in County Fermanagh, burning mansions belonging to those Costello described as 'his enemies' and driving their cattle into the bogs, hills and woodland.

In 1667, during one of these cattle raids in Killasser, Costello and his men were driving the cattle towards Barnalyra Wood when they were ambushed at a crossing on the River Moy. Costello was killed by an English officer with what was described at the time as 'a lucky shot'. However, the rest of his men managed to escape, including his second in command, Captain Nangle. Costello's head was sent to Dublin and displayed on a spike for a year and a day outside St James's Prison, now the Guinness Brewery. The inscription on a plaque above his head read 'The Scourge of Mayo'.

Captain Gallagher

Captain Gallagher was born in Bonniconlon but reared in Derryronane near Swinford by his aunt. In many ways he was Ireland's answer to Dick Turpin, a folk hero and a champion of the peasant classes who suffered injustice and oppression at the hands of the rich and ruling classes.

He led a small band of men armed with blunderbusses and they operated over quite a wide area, stretching from Bonniconlon to Swinford, including Attymass, Lough Talt and Foxford. Eventually they began raiding mail coaches as well as wealthy landowners and travellers throughout eastern Mayo and parts of southern County Sligo and western County Roscommon. His attacks on landowners were especially widely known and, in one reported incident, he and his men raided the home of an extremely unpopular landlord in Killasser. He forced the landlord to eat half a dozen eviction notices he had recently drawn up his tenant farmers. Gallagher then escaped with silver and other valuables.

They were known to be utterly fearless and had no problem carrying out robberies in broad daylight. They also had no qualms about robbing the houses of the rich almost on a nightly basis. It was said that nowhere was beyond Gallagher's reach.

Captain Gallagher has become part of the folklore of County Mayo. His generosity to the poor, his ability to escape the clutches of the redcoats and his retreat to the Ox Mountains are legendary. The people of Swinford will recall that one of Gallagher's hiding places was Barnalyra Wood, and it has been suggested that he even had a house on Glass Island near Pontoon.

Amongst the stories told about Gallagher's exploits, there is one concerning a shop in Foxford. Apparently the shop was robbed on a regular basis, despite the owner hiring a night-watchman; the culprit always seemed to just fade away. Captain Gallagher offered his services and hid in a large chest in a dark corner of the shop. The nightwatchman arrived shortly after-wards and, instead of standing guard, he proceeded to rob the place. Gallagher jumped out of the box and held him captive until the shopkeeper had him tied up. It turned out it was the nightwatchman who was the thief all along.

Another story tells us of a woman who was coming home from the fair in Tubbercurry. She had been there to sell her house cow so she could pay her rent to her landlord. We all know how important that cow must have been to her family as it would have supplied milk, butter, cheese and buttermilk. The poor woman must have been in a desperate situation if she found herself forced to sell it.

Nightfall was fast approaching and she was passing through a windy gap when all of a sudden she saw a dark shadow coming towards her. A person spoke, asking her where she was going at this time of day and why did she seem to be in such a hurry.

'I'm trying to get home before dark, sir. It's on account of Captain Gallagher; I'm afraid he might rob me of what little I have, sir.'

Captain Gallagher questioned her and upon finding out her reason for going to the fair he gave her the full price of the cow so she could buy a new one and he also gave her the money to pay her rent to the landlord. He told her to go safely home and tell whoever she knew that Captain Gallagher was not as bad as he was painted out to be.

Captain Gallagher's reign was finally ended when his band of men were captured near Westport. Gallagher escaped but was finally captured near Foxford. According to one story, he was staying in a house where he was recovering from an illness. He was given a meal that had been laced with poteen and upon falling into a deep sleep the people of the house tied him up and sent word to the redcoats in Foxford. Another version blames a jealous neighbour and, in order to save his host, Gallagher surrendered. Whichever version you believe, the final outcome remains the same. The redcoats alerted Ballina, Swinford and Castlebar, a huge force turned up and Gallagher, already bound, was taken to Castlebar to be hanged after a hasty sham trial.

His execution in 1818 is said to have been the last public hanging to take place on the hanging tree opposite Daly's Hotel on the Mall in Castlebar.

Charles Gavan Duffy, the Young Irelander, wrote a ballad called 'The Rapparees':

Now Sassenach and Cromweller, take heed of what I say,
Keep down your black and angry looks that scorn us night and day;
For there's a just and wrathful Judge that every action sees,
And he'll make strong, to right our wrong, the faithful Rapparees.

AN GORTA MÓR /
THE GREAT FAMINE
1845–1850

Ireland has suffered the devastating effects of famine many times during her history. The Great Famine, or *An Gorta Mór*, is the most important event in modern Irish history and the actions of the government of the day compounded its effects. The failure of the potato crop was unprecedented and led to the deaths of more than 1.5 million people and mass emigration on a scale never seen before or since. It was a time that most Irish people rarely talk about. Some remember it as a famine; however, others still refer to it as 'The Great Starvation' for when there is food enough to export there should be no famine.

> God sent a curse upon the land because her sons were slaves.
> The rich earth brought forth rottenness, and gardens became graves,
> The green crops withered in the fields, all blackened by the curse,
> And wedding gay and dance gave way to coffin and to hearse.
>
> (Anon., 1849)

Féar Gortach

'*Féar gortach*' means 'hungry grass'. This is a patch of dead grass that pops up where someone has died violently, according to some, while others say it happens where someone has died of hunger specifically. There are those who suggest that it's a spot where a corpse has lain on the way to its final resting place, or even where they still lie, covered by grass, a reminder of the famine. There are even those who say that it may be a fairy curse. Whatever the reason, the grass becomes a predator.

Have you ever been walking down a green grassy *bóithrín* (the Irish term for a small road with room for one cow) on a bright sunny day when you were suddenly overtaken by a hunger so strong you almost passed out? Believe me, it's happened and a good Irishman would immediately know why and what to do. Anyone who walks or passes over the *féar gortach* in Irish, will suddenly become hungry beyond reason, even if they have just been well fed. Those who live near patches of such grass have been known to keep extra food on hand in the case of afflicted travellers knocking on their door. No other side effects are known.

Sometimes you might even hear some of the older folk say, 'The *féar gortach* is on me', meaning they are feeling very hungry. When we were young children we were told to always have a biscuit or a piece of bread in our pockets when going out for a walk just in case the *féar gortach* came on us. However, if you didn't have a biscuit you could always suck on a shoelace.

As an adult when I visit somewhere like the famine village over in Achill, I place a piece of bread and pour a little of what I have to drink onto the ground as an offering to the spirits of the place.

The Fear Gorta

When we were children we were told the story of the *Fear Gorta* or the 'Man of Hunger'. He was a tall thin man dressed in black, raggedy clothes. He travelled around County Mayo, going from place to place, village to village and town to town during times of famine. It was said that when he knocked on your door you had to welcome him as you would a stranger and offer him a little food

The Fir Gorta.

and drink even though food was extremely hard to come by during the famine. For this reason many would hide behind closed doors, some would deny him any food or drink and some would even chase him from the door. For these people there would be no hope; they had sealed their fate – death by starvation.

Those who spared a small piece of potato or a drop of milk, even if that was all the family had, or those who genuinely had nothing except the offer of a welcome hand would be thanked by the *Fear Gorta* for their generosity. He would then politely refuse their offer and take his leave of them. However, before he left he would say, 'Because of your generosity and your honest welcome today you will be truly blessed. Neither you nor your family will ever die of the hunger. Tell no others of what has passed here but from this day forth your pot will never be empty, your jug will never run dry.' In the morning the woman of the house would go to the pot, where she would find a great big potato, more than enough to feed the whole family, and a jug that was brimming over with fresh, creamy milk. It would be the same each morning and the family would survive the famine.

Ireland has traditionally been known as the 'land of a thousand welcomes'; however, I wonder how many of us would welcome a stranger to our door today with an offer of a hot meal and a warm drink?

3

THE LEGENDS
OF INISHKEA
AND INISHGLORA

INISHKEA

The Inishkea Islands are situated off the north Mayo coast and consist of Inishkea North and Inishkea South. They are also known as the Goose Islands in Irish (*Inis Gé*).

The islands were named after a woman called Kea who founded a small community of nuns there. However, the inhabitant I wish to tell you about is a magical crane. It is said that he has been on the island since the beginning of time, perched high up on a rock looking out over the Atlantic Ocean. He keeps a lonely vigil; never visited by any of his own kind, he ignores all other birds. Life passes him by like a fog drifting in from the sea and folklore tells us that he will continue his vigil until the end of time.

INISHGLORA

It is said that bodies buried on the Island of Inishglora, situated off the coast of North Mayo, do not decompose because the air and soil have magical powers that prevent decay. In times past, bodies were taken to the island and left lying above ground in the open air. It was said that they remained unchanged and that even their nails and hair grew quite naturally so that years later a person could return to the Island and still recognise not only their father and grandfather but even their ancestors. It is claimed that this was true until the monks left the island (R. Nolan, 1997).

Gerald of Wales, a member of the aristocratic Norman family of the Fitzgeralds, was a visitor to Ireland in the twelfth century. He wrote:

> In this island human corpses are not buried and do not putrefy, but are placed in the open and remain without corruption. Here men see with some wonder and recognise their grandfathers, great grandfathers, and great, great grandfathers and a long line of ancestors.
>
> (Wright, T. (ed.), *The historical works of Giraldus Cambrensis*)

It was also claimed that the sand and clay from the island would banish rats and mice and that this would work even if soil was taken to use on the mainland. Gerald of Wales went on to write:

> There is another remarkable thing about this island. While the whole of Ireland is infested with mice, there is not a single mouse here. For no mouse is bred here, nor does one live if it be brought in. If by any chance it is brought in, it makes straight for the nearest point of the sea and throws itself in; if it be prevented, it dies on the spot.
>
> (Wright, T. (ed.), *The historical works of Giraldus Cambrensis*)

Another legend tells us that there was a tradition that infertile couples who did a station on the island would be blessed with a family. Having done the station, they retired to a special bed on the island. Maybe we can think of it as an early fertility clinic. There is also a story told about a curious blackbird that visits Inishglora and apparently the only other place it's seen is Sceilig Mhicil.

The island is uninhabited today; if you visit you will find the ruins of old buildings, including the two churches (one for men, the other for women). There are some beehive huts that were used by the monks, and perhaps even predate the arrival of Christianity, and there is a well known as St Brendan's Well, which has steps leading down to it. The well has its own superstition associated with it, which states that if a woman takes water from it, the water will turn to blood and this blood will be full of worms. This has been put to the test and has been found to be untrue.

Could this superstition have been created for practical reasons? Lonely monks going down the steps into a dark place might have meet lonely nuns fetching water and of course we all know what can happen then, don't we? 'It was the waters' fault' was the cry. So there you have it: the women had to be kept away from the well.

You will still find garden herbs, introduced by the monks and nuns hundreds of years ago, growing wild all over the island and locals say that the herbs will grow until the end of time. Who can say? Maybe they will.

The Children of Lir

Once upon a time long, long ago there lived a king who ruled the sea and his name was Lir. He had a beautiful wife called Eva, with whom he was to have four children. The eldest son was called Aodh, they had a daughter called Fionnuala and twin boys, Fiachra and Conn. Unfortunately their mother died whilst giving birth to the twins, leaving Lir and his children heartbroken. Lir needed to re-marry so his children could have a mother and he could have some company, so he married Eva's sister, Aoife. Unknown to Lir, Aoife was an evil witch.

At first all seemed to go well. Aoife appeared to love the children and she was a good wife to Lir. However, it was not to last. Soon Aoife began to resent the children and she became jealous of the time that the king spent with them. One day she decided that she had had enough; the only way she was going to get the attention she deserved from Lir was to rid herself of these troublesome children. Aoife suggested that the children pay a visit to their grandfather. On the way, they stopped by a lake where she encouraged them to go for a swim. Due to the fact that their father was the king of the sea, the children had been born with gills and webbing between their fingers and toes, so they loved the water and were having a great time happily splashing each other. They didn't notice that their stepmother was now standing at the water's edge wearing their father's magic cloak.

'For too long you have stood between me and your father, but no more for now I will be rid of you,' Aoife screamed.

'We can't be killed by the likes of you,' Aodh replied, 'we are the children of Lir and if you harm us then our ghosts will haunt you until the end of time.'

'Ohhh, I'm not going to kill you,' she cried. 'I have something far worse planned for you.'

Aoife bowed her head and began to cast a spell. The children looked at each other in fear as they saw a dark circle begin to envelop them on the water. Aoife opened her cloak and from within a great fireball emerged and hurtled towards them, destroying everything in its wake. When the fireball hit the water, steam began to rise up around the children. As the steam rose, they began to lose all feeling in their legs and arms and their sight faded. They were soon to regain their sight, only to see Aoife standing at the water's edge, laughing at them. Aodh tried to raise his arm in order to attack her but for some reason he just started to furiously splash the water. He turned to his brothers and sister and it was then he realised that they had all been turned into the most beautiful swans ever seen.

Aoife screamed at them and told them that she had cursed them with a spell. They were to spend nine hundred years as swans: three hundred on Lough Derravaragh, three hundred on the straits of Moyle and three hundred on the isle of Inishglora. To end the spell they would have to hear the bell of the new God.

'I leave you with your voices, however, and they will be the most beautiful singing voices ever heard,' she said.

When Aoife arrived back home, Lir was frantic. He had not known about the trip and had been searching for his children all day. Aoife told him that they had been attacked and killed by wild boars. Aoife in her triumph had not noticed that the children had followed her back and Fionnuala, now in swan form, approached her father and told him what Aoife had done. Lir was furious and banished Aoife into exile, turning her into a crane, the bird symbolising of death in Celtic lore.

The children spent the first three hundred years on the lake and their father made sure that their time was spent as happily as it could be. The next three hundred years began and the swans left for the straits of Moyle, never to see their father again.

Children of Lir

Unfortunately, without the power of their father's love, their time on the northern straits of Moyle was less joyous. There were frequent storms and it was very cold but at least they survived and were still together.

After another three hundred years they left the cold straits and flew over the land, looking down at where their father's fort had been but by now it was in ruins. The time of the Tuatha Dé Danann had ended and they began to weep. Travelling west, they arrived at Inishglora and found refuge on a saltwater lake. Here time passed slowly.

One day an old man visited the lake and the children asked him if he was a follower of the new God. The man was startled; he had heard the legend of the children of Lir but always believed it to be just a story. He asked them if they were the children of Lir and they told him that they were.

'Are you a holy man?' asked Fiachra.

'I am,' replied the old man.

The children realised that the time of their entrapment was coming to an end. The holy man began to tell them of his new God and of a man called Patrick. The children became excited as they knew that this was the new God that their stepmother had told them about. They stayed with the holy man for many years and were given sanctuary in a small church he had built. The holy man had spent years melting down old bits of metal that he found, with which he intended to make a bell to put onto the top of the church. The time came and the bell was completed and ready to be rung when disaster struck.

A warrior dressed in armour arrived on the island. He entered the church and demanded the swans he had heard about. He was Liargen, the King of Connacht, and his wife had been told of the beautiful singing voices of the swans.

'My wife desires those swans and I will have them,' he said. 'Hand them over or I will tear this church to the ground.'

Fionnuala looked at the holy man and, not wishing any harm to come to the old man, told the king that they would go away with him. Liargen was amazed to hear her speak but soon composed himself and ordered his men to take the children. They were being loaded onto a carriage when the church bell tolled loudly. Time stood still. Suddenly a great white mist blew in off the nearby lake and enveloped the children as it had done nine hundred years before. The mist changed into all of the colours of the rainbow before a great wind blew it away. As it disappeared, the men saw that the children had been transformed back into human form. Liagren fled, leaving the children behind, and never returned. The children began to age rapidly and the holy man knew that they would soon die so he quickly baptised them.

However, before they finally turned to dust, Fionnuala gave instructions for their burial. She asked for a wide grave to be dug near the little church and the children of Lir were buried together as Fionnuala had directed: Conn at her right hand, Fiachra at her left and Aodh standing before her face. They were buried on Inishglora and tradition tells us that while the Gaughan family lived on the island they kept the grave covered with white stones. It is still tended to this day by one of the locals who travels across from the mainland (R. Nolan, 1997).

The holy man was St Brendan.

One last interesting point: it is claimed that in the past all ships sailing by the island lowered their topsails to honour St Brendan the Navigator who founded the settlement there. So next time you see one of the local boats lowering their sails or sounding their horns, you'll know why.

The God Stone of Inishkea or The Naomhóg

In 1851, Robert Jocelyn, the third Earl of Rodan and a prominent protestant Tory, wrote about the stone idol of Inishkea, also known as the *Naomhóg*. He referred to the islanders as a bunch of heathens, linking their use of the Irish language and Celtic traditions with ignorance and popery he believed set the seeds for the Great Famine of 1845.

Jocelyn recorded that the population of Inishkea numbered around four hundred. They supported themselves with a diet of fish, potato crops, shellfish and seaweed. Ruled over by their own king, they were to all intents and purpose self-sufficient and lived by their own self-imposed laws. They had been baptised into the Church by the clergy who visited from the mainland occasionally and they made rare visits to worship in the king's house and at the holy well, which they called 'Derivla', but despite all this, they continued to practise their traditional religion.

According to Jocelyn, the people of the islands worshipped a stone idol which was dressed in flannel and cared for by a priest-ess. The origin of this idol and its early history has long been forgotten but it is said to have had immense power. The island-ers prayed to it in times of sickness and its power was invoked in order to manipulate the weather. When they saw a ship in the distance, it is alleged that they would pray for a storm and that the resulting heavy seas would smash the helpless ship against the rocks. They would then plunder the contents and dispose of survi-vors. Conversely, the islanders would pray to the stone idol when the seas were choppy in order to calm the waves so they could go fishing or visit the mainland.

There are a number of different stories told about the power of the stone idol. One stormy day an island man was so sick that his wife believed he was not long for this world. Although she had prayed to the idol to restore him to health, it was to no avail. She decided to send for the priest from the mainland to see if he could help him; if not, he could at least administer the last rites. Unfortunately, there was an incredible storm brewing and the islanders were scared of putting to sea without the stone idol to protect them on their voyage. They placed the idol in the boat and set off for the mainland. They successfully made the voyage and declared to the astonished priest that it was the presence of the idol that ensured their safety. The sick man recovered and this was also attributed to the power of the *Naomhóg*.

Another story relates how a number of pirates landed upon South Island and, finding very little plunder, decided to set fire to all the cottages. They burned very easily as they were mainly constructed of timber and straw – all except one, that is. This one would not burn no matter what they did to it. Every time they lit a fire, it promptly went out. The leader of the pirates was incensed by this and, suspecting witchcraft, he ordered the cottage to be searched. He had heard rumours about the power of a stone idol that was in the possession of the islanders and when his men appeared carrying the *Naomhóg*, he gave orders that it should be smashed. This would put an end to the raising of storms and the destruction of ships that he considered his own; it would also prevent the islanders from seeking their revenge upon him for his actions that day.

The pirates, laughing, returned to their ship and sailed away, never to return. The islanders collected all the broken pieces of the stone idol, tied them together with strips of leather and dressed the idol in a suit of red flannel to keep it warm. This flannel was then replaced every New Year. No one is sure whether the treatment by the pirates had any long-lasting effect on the idol but the islanders still held it in great regard (C. Otway, 1841).

I wonder if *Naomhóg* refers to little Niamh, daughter of the King of the Sea, Manannán Mac Lir, who took Oisín to Tír na nÓg? Her father had power over the sea so it might not be too much of a stretch of the imagination to assume that his daughter would have the same powers to command the waves and storms. Could it be that the red flannel suit was in fact a dress?

There is also a story that was told to an English traveller in 1959. He was told that God Stone was associated with potato fertility during the famine of 1845–50 and that the islanders from South Inishkea stole the idol from the islanders of North Island. It was supposedly thrown into the sea by a Catholic priest called Father O'Reilly in the 1890s. He died shortly afterwards and the islanders swear it was a direct result of his attempted destruction of the idol (T. White, 1959).

However, on the night of the 28 October 1927 the power of the sea was to prove deadly. It is said that even the oldest fisherman can be surprised at the sudden anger shown by the sea. On this night, thirty currachs set out on a fishing expedition, each manned by two men. It was a dark night but the sea had been calm all that day and although the barometers showed low pressure they decided to take a chance. Ten of those young men would pay the ultimate price just over an hour after setting out: eight men from South Island and two from North Island were swept to their death.

Like a screaming banshee the hurricane came out of the night, tossing their boats as if they were made of nothing more than paper. It was said afterwards that many more would have died had it not been for their uncanny ability to read the weather. They sensed a change in the air and turned their boats for home, shouting to others to do the same; those who reacted quickly were saved, their boats thrown up onto the shore by the power of the waves. The others were not so lucky; the storm was so bad that nothing could be done to save them. Six currachs didn't manage to reach land and of the twelve young men on these currachs, only two were saved: brothers John and Anthony Meenaghan. The people of Inishkea waited on the shore all night, hoping beyond hope that the other ten young men would return home, but when the following morning dawned their hopes were dashed. They found the broken remains of four currachs and one unbroken. Only one body was found that day: that of John Reilly, who had been accompanied by his younger brother, 14-year-old Terry. As the days progressed more bodies were found, washed up on the shores of the mainland one by one, sometimes only identifiable by their clothing or their boots.

The storm was so bad that the families of the deceased were unable to get to Falmore cemetery to attend the funerals of their loved ones. Michael Keane's body was never found. If that wasn't bad enough, five years later two more fishermen from North Island were drowned. One of these, Michael Lavelle, was never found. A monument with their twelve names on it was erected in Falmore. In the 1930s the families of both islands left for the mainland. They still retain the right to their properties on the islands and some of those families are still fishermen (Nolan, R, 1997).

The islands now lie empty except for the birds, seals and the odd donkey. Tourists visit when the weather allows and they wander the islands, looking at the abandoned cottages and the ruins of the old church and schoolhouse. I have been there myself and felt an eerie silence as the wind kissed my cheek, the only sounds coming from the gulls and the gentle grazing of the few animals left there. It was a very moving and emotional experience and I couldn't help but feel a lump in my throat as I read the names of those poor young men who fought the sea that dark October night and lost. May all those brave seafarers rest in peace.

Poteen

It has been said that poteen has been produced in Ireland ever since the first potato was plucked from the ground. The name 'poteen' means 'little pot' and is supposed to reflect its small-scale production.

According to legend, St Patrick was said to have been responsible for introducing poteen to Ireland in the fifth century AD. Having run out of mass wine, he brewed up the first batch of poteen. However, I would suggest that this is a complete fabrication that has more to do with the fact that Christian monks recorded the practice of poteen-making in written form and, as with a lot of other myths concerning St Patrick, has since become part of Irish folklore.

In fact one of the earliest records of distilling aqua vitae, or the water of life, also has a religious connection. In the Exchequer Rolls of 1494, it was recorded that eight bolls of malt were delivered to Friar John Cor to make whiskey. Distilled spirits were commonly made in monasteries for medical purposes and were often pre-scribed for the preservation of good health and as a general cure-all. There were monastic distilleries recorded in Ireland in the late twelfth century. The medical benefits were formally endorsed in 1505 when the Guild of Surgeon Barbers was granted a monopoly over the manufacture of aqua vitae, which they used when carry-ing out surgical procedures.

Of course there have been many in the medical profession who have condemned poteen as highly dangerous and warned of the very real threat of alcohol poisoning, as well as claiming that it was responsible for huge problems with alcoholism in rural Ireland. They also pointed out the increase in mental illness and it was suggested at one time that more than half the people in the mental asylum in County Mayo were there because of the effects of poteen-drinking. However, in 1730, one doctor claimed that drinking poteen to the point of intoxication held off old age, aided digestion, enlightened the heart and quickened the mind. I would not recommend following this advice, folks.

In Ireland we hold a wake for someone who has died. This practice was said to have started because of the after-effects of poteen. It was said that people didn't know if those who were lying as if dead were just unconscious or were actually dead so they used to wait up at night for them to wake up, hence the name. A more recent story, which is probably a myth, is that wakes began because of the frequent lead poisoning suffered by people drinking from pewter tankards. One of the symptoms of lead poisoning is that of a catatonic state that resembles death, from which you would hopefully recover in anything from a few hours to a couple of days. It was for this reason that a burial was delayed to give the poor unfortunate a chance to wake up. I'd make your own mind up about that one.

It was in 1661 that King Charles II, attempting to rebuild the post-war treasury, decided to introduce a charge on spirits. In Ireland private stills were outlawed and a large section of the Irish population became criminals at the stroke of a pen. The Irish ignored the tax and the making of poteen went underground. In 1770, the English tried to clamp down on the trade once again but it did very little to slow down production and poteen-making took off as a thriving cottage industry.

The stills were moved from cottage to barn, then to small shacks in the hills and mountains. Some enterprising individuals set up stills in ancient burial chambers (I wonder if that's why they are called spirits), some set up on small islands in the middle of lakes, so they could see the Gardaí coming, and one fellow even had his still set up on a small boat on a lough – it was said that for many years he was able to out-row the local Gardaí.

There is a wealth of folklore regarding poteen.

Leprechauns are frequently found in a drunken state caused by poteen. Poteen made in fairy mounds is seen as magical. It was used for curing painful rheumatic joints and half a cup given morning and night was said to be a cure for all ailments. It was said to be especially potent if a housewife left fresh cream and bread by a fairy mound at night and asked the fairies for a cure for illness. The fairies would then leave a cup of poteen outside the cottage door to heal the sick.

Poteen made from the water of a fairy spring or a sacred well also gave it healing properties and it was used by wise women like Biddy Early in medicinal cures.

Drinking poteen on a fairy hill at night will call the fairies to you. In exchange for a drink they are said to grant you a wish. However, give them too much and you may end up as their permanent guest. Drinking poteen is also said to be responsible for hallucinations. I'm saying nothing.

The Achill islanders once referred to poteen simply as 'Inishkea' because of the superior quality and flavour of poteen produced on the islands. In fact they suggested that the islanders of Inishkea should be declared saints because of their skill. The reasons given for the quality of this illegal produce included the remote location of Inishkea, which enabled the still owners to take their time in distilling the alcohol without fear of interruption by the customs man or the Gardaí. Well, you should never hurry a good thing.

Another reason for superior poteen was that it was distilled in copper stills which were far better than the tin stills used on the mainland. These stills were often hidden in the caves on the western side of the island, well away from the prying eyes of unwelcome visitors, and were so valuable they were handed down from father to son. Inishkea islanders had very limited sources of income. Fishing and poteen provided them with products that could be sold or traded on the mainland and the sale of poteen found willing buyers within the clergy (both Catholic and Protestant) and the Gardaí. There were always customers on Achill Island who eagerly awaited a new batch of poteen. Unfortunately this was to lead to a great tragedy in 1898 when an Inishkea islander and his daughter were lost at sea while rowing to Achill with a cargo of poteen. This led to three members of the RIC (Royal Irish Constabulary) being stationed on the island (R. Nolan, 1997).

Eventually the Church declared the drinking of poteen a sin. In the 1950s, the Lord Bishop of Clogher, Most Revd Dr O'Callaghan, declared it to be a product that led to smuggling and blamed all the troubles of Ireland on its consumption. One man arrested for its production said, 'The devil drove me to it, yer Honour'. He was convicted and fined a total of £33.

4

TADHG DALL O'HUIGINN: THE MATCHSTICK MAN OF STRAIDE

The village of Straide lies between Foxford and Castlebar in the heart of County Mayo. It was the birthplace of Michael Davitt, founder of the Land League and he is buried in the graveyard of the thirteenth-century friary. As you walk around the cemetery you will see an old grave marker upon which is carved a matchstick man. There is no name on the marker but I strongly suspect it is the final resting place of Tadhg Dall O'Huiginn.

Tadhg Dall O'Huiginn was a bardic poet and scholar who came from a long line of distinguished Irish poets. He received his training within his family and may also have received training in the bardic school in Ceall Cluaine (in County Galway) where a number of his family had been trained. The attachment of 'Dall' to his name suggests that he had a visual impairment and he may have been blind in one or both eyes, although it has been suggested that he may not have been completely blind.

Tadhg was a wealthy man by today's standards as he owned land and property throughout Sligo and Mayo that amounted to hundreds of acres and he enjoyed a very comfortable lifestyle. As a poet of note, he was welcomed in all the great houses of Ireland, where he spent many weeks being wined and dined by his hosts. It was the custom in ancient Ireland for the poets to compose poems that spoke of the hospitality and greatness of the nobility. These poems could make or break the reputation of the ruling chieftains, so poets were treated extremely well. The treatment of the bard would then be reflected in what he wrote and the reputation of the chieftain would be enhanced in the eyes of all through the public reading of the poetry or verse. This made Tadhg an extremely powerful man in the Ireland of his day in much the same way as a highly influential journalist would be considered in the Ireland of today.

However, Tadhg was also said to have a sharp tongue and the gift of satire and it was this that cost him his life. Tadhg had visited Cormac O'Hara of the O'Hara Buí (Yellow) and received such a welcome and was treated so well that he wrote a poem that praised the O'Hara Buí to the highest. The poem became the talk of Connacht and made the O'Hara Buí famous for their prowess in battle, their lineage and genealogy, and their magnificent hospitality.

In Connacht there was another branch of the O'Haras. They were known as O'Hara Rua (Red) and when they heard of this poem they were extremely displeased. They were already in contention with O'Huiginn regarding the title to some land and this insult to their line just heightened their intense dislike of him, so they decided to seek retribution. One night, when Tadhg was away on his travels, the O'Hara Rua decided to pay a visit to his house. Six of the O'Hara Rua broke in and stole food and drink before leaving.

This led to even greater animosity between the O'Hara Rua and O'Huiginn and O'Huiginn got his retribution by writing a poem ridiculing the six. In a time when there were no televisions or newspapers, the poetry of the bard was eagerly awaited by the people and was quickly spread throughout the land. O'Huiginn's poem made the O'Hara Rua the laughing stock of the countryside. No matter where they went, people pointed and sniggered. At last they could take no more and they decided to kill Tadhg O'Huiginn.

They hatched a plan, set an ambush and lay in wait for him one Sunday in 1591 when they knew he was returning home. He managed to escape and fled on horseback to the nearby Friary of Corpus Christi, where he claimed sanctuary, believing that this would give him the protection of God's house. Unfortunately for Tadhg, the prior of the friary was an O'Hara who was related to the O'Hara Rua. He turned his back on O'Huiginn and refused to help him. Tadhg was pulled from the friary and died a horrifying death; the O'Hara Rua cut out his tongue, then slit his throat. They also gave orders that his wife and child were to be murdered.

The O'Hara Rua responsible for these horrendous acts were eventually captured and taken to Sligo, where they were tried for the murders in 1593, but they were released due to the apparent lack of witnesses and evidence.

Tradition suggests that Tadhg Dall O'Huiginn was buried in the grounds of Straide Friary in County Mayo and I suspect that it is his grave that is marked by the grave marker that shows a carving of a matchstick man.

5

THE LOVE FLOWER

In County Mayo in the west of Ireland, there is a flower called the love daffodil. Most daffodils bloom in spring, a beautiful yellow, and they lift their heads to the sun, which they follow until it sets in the west. The daffodil then slowly closes its petals and droops its head toward the ground until the sun rises the next morning.

The love daffodil pushes through the snow in January. It is rocked by cold winds and the sun that shines down on it is an icy sun. The love daffodil is red in colour and folklore will tell you that if you find it on a clear frosty night when the moon is full, you will see blood dripping from its petals onto the snow-covered ground. You may ask why there is such a sad flower growing alone in the middle of winter before even the crocus heralds the coming spring.

Well, it all happened long, long ago, when Ireland was a much simpler place than it is now. There was a rich farmer whose wife gave birth to a beautiful baby girl. They called her Caithleen. Caithleen inherited her good looks from her mother but she inherited her father's brains, which was a good thing for her mother was extremely vain and shallow.

Everywhere her father went, Caithleen would follow, listening to every word that was spoken. The workers on the farm loved her because she never forgot their names. She treated everyone from the oldest to the youngest the same. The girls were jealous of her long black hair, her dark eyes and her skin, which was as smooth as velvet, and yet they still loved her. The boys all loved her too and would blush and stutter in front of her, not knowing how to act or how speak to one as beautiful as her.

Caithleen's mother watched all of this and became more and more envious of her daughter. The more the mother's beauty faded the more she made plans to be rid of Caithleen so that once again she would be called the most beautiful in all of Ireland. One day, as Caithleen was away on some errand, she spoke to her husband.

'Husband,' she said, 'you are a rich man in many ways.'

He nodded, tapping his pipe on the heel of his boot. 'I have been blessed many times over; I have a beautiful wife, a daughter I love and land that is fertile. Yes, I am a very lucky man.'

She watched him slyly as he gazed into the fire. 'I hear there are thieves and murderers on the roads looking for beautiful young girls to take for ransom,' she said.

Her husband jumped up. 'Ransom?' he said in horror.

'Yes, husband, all the gold you can find and when they get it they still kill the poor young girls,' she replied.

'I won't let that happen to our Caithleen,' said the husband, 'I'll hire men to protect her.'

'That won't stop them; they are armed and they are killers,' replied the mother.

'What are we to do then?' said the husband.

This was exactly what the evil wife wanted to hear. She turned her face away so he wouldn't see the look of glee on her face. In a sad voice she said, 'For her own good she must be locked up in the cellar where no one will ever find her.'

'Never,' he cried, 'Caithleen is like a flower; she needs the rain on her face and the warm summer sun to blossom. I'll have to think about this.'

For the next month he thought long and hard. His wife was going mad wondering what he was going to do until one day he spoke, 'I have made up my mind; I will build a room on top of the house. Caithleen will be able to see all the countryside but no one will be able to see her. In this way she will be safe.'

Caithleen wasn't happy with this at all but as she loved her father and obeyed him in all things she settled into her room at the top of the house. As the seasons came and went, Caithleen saw the bluebells of spring, the roses blooming in the summer, the golden fields of wheat in the autumn and when the land went to sleep in the winter, she watched the snow fall.

The years passed and Caithleen grew even more beautiful while her mother, with her sly evil ways, turned into a cranky and bitter auld woman. Everywhere she went, people kept asking about her daughter and never once mentioned how beautiful the mother was.

One winter's day her husband said that he was going to have the thatch on the roof repaired. Fear gripped his wife's heart and she gripped his arm with bony little fingers.

'If you get the roof repaired the thatcher will climb up onto the roof and if he sees Caithleen he will tell the whole country,' she cried in alarm.

Her husband had grown older than his years for he missed having his daughter following him around the farm. He missed talking to her about the things that happened each day and watching her laugh with the workers and yet he still managed to smile.

'Don't be worrying wife; I've thought of everything,' he said.

The next morning as the sun was climbing in a frosty sky, Caithleen was woken by the sound of singing. She looked out of her window and saw a young man about her own age working away, pulling out old thatch and replacing it with new. His hair was the colour of the straw. He sang of the flight of the swallow and the sound carried her to where the bird soared and, knowing the song, she joined in.

'You have beautiful voice,' he said when the song had finished.

Caithleen blushed. 'Thank you,' she said, 'so have you. I've not seen you around here before.'

With nimble feet he climbed the roof to where she stood at the window. 'I'm from the next county,' he said with a wide and happy smile, 'my name is Seamus.'

Caithleen saw that his eyes were a misty grey. He was blind.

'Be careful,' she cried, worried, 'you might slip.'

Seamus stood, as sure-footed as a mountain goat. His smile grew even wider. 'I haven't fallen off a roof yet and I'm the best thatcher in all of Ireland.'

Caithleen smiled. 'You're very sure of yourself,' she said.

Seamus grinned. 'I have to get back to work or I'll have no job and you'll get into trouble if they catch you talking to me.'

Caithleen blushed.

'Yes, I'd better, but be careful,' she said.

Over the next few days and weeks, Caithleen and Seamus would meet and talk and sing. The funny thing was no one in or around the house could hear them, yet people would stop work in the fields and listen to the sound of beautiful music and wonder what kind of new bird had come to Ireland.

One morning Seamus climbed up the roof. It was a grey day and the snow fell gently onto the thatch. Caithleen stood by her window waiting.

'It's my last day, Caithleen. I've come to say farewell.'

She wiped away the tears that ran down her face. Caithleen had fallen deeply in love with the handsome blind thatcher and tried to think of a way to stop him leaving.

'I've brought you a present,' he said. He held out his hand and in it was a flower. 'It's the first flower of spring.'

The yellow flower shone brightly against the white snowflakes that fell around him. Caithleen reached out and in that brief moment their hands touched.

'Caithleen, you have the most beautiful voice and when I hear you sing I can feel how much you care. At night I dream of what you might look like. I wonder, before I go could I touch your face, just once?'

Wordlessly, Caithleen reached out and took his hand. She guided it to her cheek. His touch was as light as a feather; he traced her hair, the shape of her eyes, her nose. His fingers lingered on her lips and gently she kissed each one.

'What's going on?'

Caithleen's mother strode into the room and seeing her daughter about to kiss the blind Thatcher she screamed, 'Get away from her.'

She dragged Caithleen away from the window and with a great push she threw Seamus backwards. He tried to keep his balance but the snow, now thick upon the roof made it too slippery. Pushing her mother away, Caithleen leaned out the window and watched her beloved slip over the side. Beneath him was the last of the straw for the roof held together by stakes stuck in the ground.

His last word before his body was impaled was her name, 'Caithleen'.

With a cry of utter despair, she leapt from the window, still clutching the daffodil. Down, down, she slipped, her eyes never leaving the body of Seamus. Her father found them, both impaled on the same stake, face-to-face, their lips touching. Between them lay the daffodil covered with their blood. With a broken heart,

he buried them side by side on the hillside overlooking the farm. It was talked about throughout the county and everyone talked of the beautiful smiles they had on their faces.

If you are suffering from a broken heart or a lost love, come to the west of Ireland in wintertime. Search for the red daffodil and if you find it, hold it close to your breast and it will heal all unhappiness.

6

SOUL GATHERERS

There are many things that hide from the light of day, things that go bump in the night. Once the sun goes down, they come creeping out of the shadows. All of us have felt a shiver up our backs, seen something out of the corner of our eye and yet when we look there is nothing there. In every country and in every culture you will find stories of those that walk or fly in the night as they seek the souls of the living. Who or what they are, only the dead know and they're not talking.

Many birds were believed to carry dead souls or were believed to be dead people incarnate. The belief in transmigration of human souls goes back to ancient times. Often these bird souls would come back with a message or warning. Storm petrels, also known as 'Mother Carey's Chickens', contained the souls of dead seamen who came to warn their brethren of approaching storms. Seagulls were also regarded as the repositories of dead souls and were not to be harmed.

Back on land, when sedge warblers sang at night and particularly at midnight, their voices were believed to be those of dead babies who chose to return temporarily from the other world to sing in order to soothe the hearts and minds of their poor, grieving mothers.

Soul Gatherers.

Magpies were regarded as the repositories of the souls of evil-minded or gossiping women. Swans contained the souls of virtuous women and they had the capability of turning back into human form and the linnet was thought to contain an unhappy soul that was trapped in the other world.

THE SEVEN WHISTLERS

These were said to be seven birds, flying together by night, whose whistle-like cries forebode disaster. (It was a common belief, particularly among seamen, that whistling was unlucky.) Sometimes the whistlers were said to be the spirits of the dead, especially those who had themselves been fishermen, returning to warn comrades of danger. When they were heard, one had to stop work at once and return home; otherwise lives would be lost. Even those who knew the cries were in fact those of curlews and similar birds still dreaded the sound and would not go out until the next day.

In one variation to this tale they were said to be seven ghostly birds that warned of death and disaster and flew alongside the banshee. Another variation suggested that the birds carry the grief-stricken souls of unbaptised babies, condemned to roam the skies forever.

The Sluagh

In Westport, County Mayo, if you take a walk in the evening just before dusk you will see and hear flocks of crows as they return home to their roosting spots on the buildings and treetops of the town. They are as much part of our town as the river that flows through it and yet I cannot but think of the other black shapes that once flew through the sky, the shapes that sent a shiver up the spine. Those shapes had a name: the *Sluagh*.

'*Sluagh*' is an Irish word meaning 'host'. The *Sluagh* are said to be evil spirits that hunt for souls. They come from the west, flying in groups like flocks of crows, watching and waiting until they feel a dying soul. It is for this reason that when someone is close to death west-facing windows are kept shut at all times. This allows the soul of the deceased to reach heaven before the *Sluagh* can intercept it. If the *Sluagh* do find a door or window left slightly open, they will enter and linger in the shadows over the dying and wait. If you are sitting nearby, you may have even hear the eerie sound of whispers as the *Sluagh* sucked the soul from the weak and dying body.

Once the stolen spirit is captured, a terrified scream will echo from the shadows and continue through the night, slowly becoming farther away before growing silent. The soul of the dying will now be joined to the unforgiving dead. Now they too are cursed to roam forever through the dark night, damned to an eternity of sorrow. It does not matter to the *Sluagh* whether the souls are innocent or evil; any soul will do. It has been suggested that one of the ways of dissuading the *Sluagh* is to sacrifice another in your place. However, if you are willing to do that then I think you are destined to join them at some point in the future.

The *Sluagh* are well known in Ireland and Scotland and the name has brought terror to those who lay on their deathbeds. They have haunted Irish folklore for as long as people have looked into the flames and allowed their imagination to take hold. On cold winter evenings, it seems an easy thing to sit by the fire with the lights out. Shapes and shadows flicker in the darkness and it is within these shadows that you will find the *Sluagh*. Stories of who and what the *Sluagh* were date back through our folklore and these stories have been handed down from generation to generation. The stories may differ slightly but the bones of the story is always the same. Be wary of the shadow in the corner. Once Christianity arrived in Ireland, the *Sluagh* were transformed into dead sinners that were once human. They were described as the souls of the darkest sinners, sinners so evil that not even the fires of the eternal flame would burn them. They were so evil that the underworld spat out their rotten souls and the earth rejected their very presence. They were cursed to soar above the earth, welded together for eternity, never to set foot or claw upon the ground.

The *Sluagh* were said to be bird-like with long, thin fingers that were webbed with leathery skin (a bit like a bat). They were said to have cape-like wings that flapped in the night, long claws that protrude from deformed legs and to smell like rotten meat. It was believed that the sound of beating wings together with this smell would alert you to their presence. If you heard a knock on the door or a nail scratching at the window, you would be wise to ignore it.

Although the *Sluagh* may be met at any time of the year, especially those times associated with the dead, they were said to be most prevalent during the long, dark nights of winter.

In modern-day Ireland stories are just that – stories – and they can be laughed at or viewed as entertainment. They are considered to be nothing more than superstition or bedtime reading, stories told by the storyteller to send children off to sleep before the sandman sprinkles his magic dust or the bogeyman crawls out to get you. However, take a minute and answer me this: have you ever lain in bed, watching shadows creep across the room when there is no light to make shadows? Have you ever heard a faraway shriek? Was it a cat? Wait a minute. It didn't sound like a cat. Oh, I know: it must be an owl. Or was it? What about the time you woke up from a deep sleep with that scary feeling that someone or something was

watching you? Sometimes you wake up in the morning feeling more tired and drained than when you went to sleep: your head hurts, your limbs ache, you feel thirsty. You think you may be coming down with something for that's what it feels like. Perhaps as you lay sleeping, the *Sluagh* came for you. Remember the shadows on the ceiling or in the corner of your eye? When you looked again they weren't there. Could it be that the *Sluagh* were feeding but left you sleeping when they heard the sound of a weaker soul? However, now they know where you are; they can hear you breathing. Lock your doors and keep your windows shut. Look to the west at night. Are they flocks of crows returning home to roost? Or are they something else, something a lot darker?

7

The Night
of the
Big Wind

The Night of the Big Wind (*Oíche na Gaoithe Móire*) is now part of Irish mythology. Accounts, both real and imaginary, of events that took place on that terrible night have been handed down through the generations. On that infamous night, nobody even knew what a hurricane was. Today we are on first-name terms with hurricanes. We can follow their approach on the television or the Internet and hopefully take some measures to protect our homes. That night the whole of Ireland was hit by the worst storm anyone had ever experienced. It was a storm of such ferocity that it became the night by which all other events were measured.

On the evening of Saturday 5 January 1839, heavy snow fell throughout Ireland. The morning was completely calm and the sky was covered with motionless dense cloud. Most of the eight million people living in Ireland at the time were preparing for Little Christmas, otherwise known as the Feast of the Epiphany.

As the morning progressed, the temperature rose well above the January average. The snow quickly melted. At that time there was no way anyone could know that there was a deep depression forming in the north Atlantic. As the warm front which covered the country gradually moved eastwards and rose in the atmosphere, it was replaced by a cold front which brought with it high winds and heavy rain. The rain began before noon in the west and spread very slowly eastwards. In County Mayo, the late afternoon turned chilly while the east of the country still enjoyed the unseasonably high temperatures experienced in Mayo earlier that day.

At dusk, wind speeds increased, conditions became colder and showers of rain and hail began to fall. At about six o'clock in the evening, the winds had become stronger and the raindrops were heavier and more like sleet. There were occasional bursts of hail-stones. Farmers became worried as they saw their winter hayricks taking a pounding and every thatched roof looked to be in danger of being ripped apart. In the towns and villages, church bells rang, dogs barked and a low rumble could be heard from the direction of the sea. By nine o'clock at night, the wind had reached gale force and continued to increase. By midnight it had reached hurricane force and remained at that level until five o'clock in the morning, when it reduced again to gale force.

During the hurricane the wind blew from the south-west, west and north-west. The hurricane had travelled thousands of miles across the Atlantic Ocean, gathering speed until it hit Ireland's west coast with such ferocity that it tore over the tops of the Cliffs of Moher. In fact it was suggested that if that barrier had not existed then Ireland would have been completely immersed in water. The sound of the sea smashing against the rocks could be heard for miles, even above the sound of the storm. Some reports tell us that the earth shook as huge boulders were tossed onto the clifftops of the Aran Islands. All this happened in the deep darkness of night. No candles or fires could remain lit in such conditions. The only light available came in the form of streaks of lightning and the blood red aurora borealis as it lit up the northern sky.

As the wind grew stronger, people were awoken by the sound of the furious wind, windows shattered by hailstones and thatched roofs were ripped off houses. Brick-built houses began to shake and chimneys, slates and sheets of lead were hurled to the ground. Many of those who died that night were killed by falling masonry and shards of glass. In Castlebar and Westport, fires erupted in

the streets. Athlone and Dublin suffered huge damage and the wind blew all the water out of the canal at Tuam. The wealthy and well-to-do did not escape unscathed. Many of the old mansions had their roofs ripped off and thousands of trees growing on their estates were lost. Due to the amount of felled timber available after the storm, timber actually became worthless as the price dropped. Many people were bankrupted by the disaster, including hundreds who had stashed their life savings up chimneys and in thatched roofs that simply disappeared in the night (*South Mayo Family Research Journal*).

From an ecological point of view the storm was a disaster. Millions of wild birds were killed, causing the near extinction of crows and jackdaws. Their traditional nesting places were wiped out and when spring eventually came, the absence of songbirds was noticeable. There was also a huge impact on our structural heritage as tower houses and churches were destroyed by the force of the weather conditions, never to be restored. Tombstones were blown over in graveyards and fallen trees caused havoc as roads became impassable, causing huge problems for deliveries, including the mail. Seawater was carried inland by the force of the storm and it flooded houses when it poured down chimneys. Seaweed and fish were also carried inland by the sea and were found miles from the seashore. It has been suggested that the most lasting reminder of that night was the smell of salt which lingered in houses for weeks.

There are people in every community who practise weather forecasting and in nineteenth-century Ireland it was no different. People would look at the behaviour of birds and animals, wind direction and insects, as well as relying on intuition of course. However, they did not have access to modern-day meteorology so unfortunately there was no way they could have predicted the storm. People began to look for other explanations.

Traditionally the fifth of January was the feast of St Ceara, when, it was believed, the fairies held a night of revelry. The fairies, they thought, caused such ructions that the storm resulted. Others believed that on that night all but a few of the fairies of Ireland left the country, never to return, and that the wind was caused by their departure. Some people even suggested that it was the night that the English fairies invaded Ireland and forced our indigenous fairies to disappear in a magic whirlwind. Of course we always seemed to blame the English for all our ills and difficulties. There was a suggestion that Freemasonry, traditionally seen by Irish Catholics as associated with demonic practices, was another possible cause. Some people were of the opinion that Freemasons had brought up the devil from hell and couldn't get him to return (*South Mayo Family Research Journal*).

The weather remained unsettled in the days after the Night of the Big Wind and occasionally the wind became gusty, causing people to fear that the storm would return. In mid-January the aurora borealis reappeared, stirring up panic.

The ill wind blew well for some people: merchants, carpenters, slaters, thatchers and builders in particular found ready work renovating public buildings and the properties of the wealthy. The poor, who could not afford to pay for such services, had to survive as best they could. The Night of the Big Wind happened prior to the introduction of government relief measures and widespread insurance. The relationship between landlord and tenant dictated that the tenant made good damage caused by storms. What little reserve of cash was held by the poor was used up in rebuilding and restocking. In many cases houses were rebuilt in sheltered locations at the bottom of hills. For many years, shelter from the wind was a primary factor in choosing a house site, until the advent of sturdier building materials. Famine followed seven years later and almost completely wiped out the class that suffered the most on the Night of the Big Wind.

As the century progressed, the Night of the Big Wind became a milestone in time. Events were referred to as happening before or after the Night of the Big Wind. Seventy years later, in 1909, old-age pensions were introduced in Ireland, entitling persons over seventy years, whose income did not exceed ten shillings per week, to an allowance of five shillings per week from the State. Those who met the means qualification, but had no documentary proof of their ages, were granted pensions if they could recall witnessing the Night of the Big Wind first-hand.

How the big wind affected people on a personal level can be illustrated by the story of Bridget Mooney. Bridget Mooney and her four young brothers were putting the finishing touches to a snowman outside their little wooden cabin in County Mayo when the hurricane struck. It was the worst storm ever recorded and made more people homeless than all the decades of the evictions which followed. If there was one place you didn't want to be on that terrible night, it was inside a wooden cabin. The day before had seen heavy snow and everything seemed normal but the following morning (Sunday), it was unusually warm and clammy. The air was so still you could hear voices floating on the air between houses more than a mile apart (T. Bunberry).

The weather began to worsen so Mrs Mooney called to her children to come inside the cabin. The Mooneys' cabin was one of thousands destroyed by the storm that night. They had no choice but to flee into the darkness in whatever clothes they had on. Like most of the Irish peasants in the nineteenth century, their clothing would not have protected them from the torrential rain and cruel freezing winds and they were soon drenched. The family sought shelter in a hedge outside Castlebar. They survived the night but the parents caught a fatal fever and died soon afterwards. The five children were now orphaned and homeless; we have no record of their fate.

Despite the advances made by science since 1839, we still do not have the means to predict or prevent the next storm of its calibre. Let us hope that one day we will be able to predict these types of severe weather conditions and take measures to protect our people from the terrible effects and aftermaths suffered in the past.

8

THE
DOBHAR CHÚ

Irish folklore is littered with legendary tales of terrible water creatures such as the aughisky, the kelpie and the selkie. However, none can be scarier than the creatures known as the '*dobhar chú*'. These creature are said to inhabit the loughs of Ireland and some people even refer to them as the Irish version of the Loch Ness Monster. Folklore suggests that they have lived in Ireland for thousands of years. Their name translates as 'water hound' though they have also been referred to as the Irish crocodile, thought to be because of their ferocious appetite and speed both in and out of the water. Witnesses have described them as being roughly seven feet long and carnivorous, with a love for human flesh. Some people even suggest that they are half wolf, half fish.

The *dobhar chú* have had a long association with County Mayo and the creatures are said to inhabit Sraheens Lough on Achill Island. There have been a large number of sightings reported although, as with their cousin 'Nessie' from across the water, these sightings have never been confirmed. One reason given for this is the creatures are migratory in nature and therefore do not live in the lough all year round.

When one is killed, it is said that its mate will swim up from the depths of the lake and avenge the killing by pursuing its attacker, killing him and often eating him. This happens because when the *dobhar chú* is about to die it gives off an eerie, high-pitched whistle to warn its mate.

There is even a religious link to the *dobhar chú*. The first sighting of the Loch Ness Monster was said to have happened in the seventh century and it was St Columba, the Irish missionary, who saw it. He was said to have challenged and overcome the monster, miraculously saving a man who was being eaten by Nessie. It was said that it was for this reason that Nessie's offspring came to inhabit the lakes of Ireland, to take revenge on the Irish people and avenge St Columba's actions. True or not, it makes an interesting story.

There are two accounts in a seventeenth-century book of encounters with the *dobhar chú* and another account is provided by a poem about a woman who was killed by the beast in the eighteenth century.

Roderick O'Flaherty, in his book, *A Description of West Connaught*, wrote about a man's encounter with what he called the Irish crocodile. The man was on the shore of Lough Mask when he saw the

head of a beast swimming in the water. He thought it was an otter. The creature seemed to look at him and then swam underwater until it reached land. Suddenly, it rushed from the water, grabbed the man by his elbow and dragged him into the lake. The man took his knife from his pocket and stabbed it, which scared the animal away. It was about the size of a greyhound, had slimy black skin and appeared to be hairless.

Old people who know the lake also reminisce about a man who was walking with his dog when he encountered one. There was a struggle between the pair and the lake monster until the creature finally went away. When the waters receded after a long period of time, they found the beast's corpse in a cave.

THE KINLOUGH TOMBSTONE

There is a tombstone in Conwell cemetery, Drummans, near Kinlough that bears a carved image of a large otter, impaled by a spear held by a hand. The first name appears as Grace, but the last one is illegible due to the ravages of the weather. The date on the tombstone is 1722. The grave is that of Grace Connolly (Gráinne Ni Conghalaigh), who was killed by a *dobhar chú* from Lough Glenade on the 24 September 1722. Like all good stories, the story of her death has been altered over the years through the retelling.

In one version, Grace Connolly was washing clothes at the edge of a Lough Glenade when she was attacked by a *dobhar chú*. Her husband, Traolach McLaughlin, heard her cries and rushed to help but by the time he got to her, she was dead. The *dobhar chú* was still there and Traolach attacked and killed it. But before it died it screamed, summoning its mate from the depths of the lough. Traolach jumped on his horse to evade the beast. A friend joined him; the *dobhar chú* chased the men across the fields and over fences, determined to take revenge on the man that had killed its mate.

After what seemed like a long chase, the two men realised that their horses couldn't outrun it. They dismounted and ducked behind a wall, as the beast hurled itself over the wall, they killed it.

Another version tells us that Grace's husband went looking for her as she had been away longer than usual and he found her mutilated body lying by the shore with the *dobhar chú* asleep on top of her. Yet another version has the *dobhar chú* feasting upon her dead corpse. In both of these versions, McLaughlin and another man, possibly his brother, shoot and kill the *dobhar chú*. As it lay dying it gave a loud scream or whistle, summoning its mate from the waters of Lough Glenade. The *dobhar chú* emerged from the lough and the chase began, determined to avenge the death of its mate.

After a long chase, during which the two men continually failed to shake off their pursuer, they were forced to stop. In this version they stopped at a blacksmith's. When the *dobhar chú* finally caught up with them, it tore straight through McLaughlin's horse and out the other side. As it emerged, McLaughlin speared the creature and killed it, finally decapitating it. The horse and creature are said to be buried near Cashelgarron fort near Benbulben, which is close to where the final fight was said to have taken place.

A version of this tale is recounted in the following poem by a contemporary but unknown author.

THE WHISTLING DOBHAR CHÚ

By Glenade Lough tradition tells, two hundred years ago
A thrilling scene enacted was to which, as years unflow,
Old men and women still relate, and while relating dread,
Some demon of its kind may yet be found within its bed.

It happened one McLaughlin lived close by the neighbouring shore,
A lovely spot, where fairies oft in rivalry wandered o'er,
A beauteous dell where prince and chief oft met in revelry,
With Frenchmen bold and warriors old to hunt the wild boar, free.

He and his wife, Grace Connolly, lived there unknown to fame,
There, years in peace, until one day from out of the Lough there came,

What brought a change in all their home and prospects too?
The water fiend, the enchanted being, the dreaded *dobhar chú*.

It was on a bright September morn, the sun scarce mountain high,
No chill or damp was in the air, all nature seemed to vie,
As if to render homage proud the cloudless sky above,
A day for mortals to discourse in luxury and love.

And whilst this gorgeous way of life in beauty did abound,
From out the vastness of the Lough stole forth the water hound,
And seized for victim her who shared McLaughlin's bed and board,
His loving wife, his more than life, whom almost he adored.

She having gone to bathe, it seems, within the water clear,
And not having returned when she might, her husband fraught
    with fear,
Hastened to where he might find her, when oh, to his surprise,
Her mangled form, still bleeding warm, lay stretched before his eyes.

Upon her bosom, snow white once, but now besmeared with gore,
The *dobhar chú* reposing was his surfeiting being o'er.
Her bowels and entrails all around tinged with a reddish hue,
'Oh, God,' he cried, ''tis hard to bear but what am I to do?'

He prayed for strength, the fiend lay still, he tottered like a child,
The blood of life within his veins surged rapidly and wild,
One long last glance at her he loved, then fast his footsteps turned
to home, while all his rage and passion fiercely burned.

He reached his house; he grasped his gun, which clenched with
    nerves of steel,
He backwards sped, upraising his arm and then one piercing dying squeal
Was heard upon the balmy air, but hark! What's that that came?
One moment next from out its depth as if to claim!

The comrade of the dying fiend with whistles long and loud
Came nigh and nigher to the spot. McLaughlin, growing cowed
Rushed to his home. His neighbours called, their counsel asked,
And flight was what they bade him do at once, and not to wait till night.

He and his brother, a sturdy pair, as brothers true when tried,
Their horses took, their homes forsook and westward fast they did ride.
One dagger sharp and long each man had for protection too
Fast pursued by that fierce brute, the whistling *Dobhar chú.*

The rocks and dells rang with its yells, the eagles screamed in dread.
The ploughman left his horses alone, the fishes too, 'tis said
Away from the mountain streams though far, went rushing to the sea,
And nature's laws did almost pause, for death or victory.

For twenty miles the gallant steeds the riders proudly bore.
With mighty strain o'er hill and dale that ne'er was seen before.
The fiend, fast closing on their tracks, his dreaded cry more shrill,
'Twas brothers try; we'll do or die on Cashelgarron Hill.

Dismounting from their panting steeds they placed them one by one
Across the path in lengthways formed within the ancient dún
And standing by the outermost horse awaiting for their foe
Their daggers raised their nerves they braced to strike that fatal blow.

Not long to wait, for nose on trail the scenting hound arrived
And through the horses with a plunge to force himself he tried,
And just as through the outermost horse he plunged his head and
    foremost part,
McLaughlin's dagger to the hilt lay buried in his heart.

'Thank God, thank God,' the brothers cried in wildness and delight,
Our humble home by Glenade Lough shall shelter us tonight
Be any doubt to what I write, go visit old Conwell,
There see the grave where sleeps the brave whose epitaph can tell.

(Anon.)

THE OTTER KING

In another version of Irish folklore, the *dobhar chú* is in fact the king of all otters, the seventh cub of an ordinary otter. It is said to be much larger than a normal otter and it never sleeps. The king of all otters is so magical that an inch of its fur would protect a man from being killed by gunshot, stop a boat from sinking or prevent a horse from being injured.

The *dobhar chú* is also often said to be accompanied by a court of ordinary otters. When captured, these beasts will grant any wish in exchange for their freedom. Their skins were prized for their ability to render a warrior invincible and were thought to provide protection against drowning. Luckily, the otter kings were hard to kill, their only vulnerable point being a small point below their chin, meaning that first you had to get past those sharp teeth.

There are also traditions of the 'King Otter', who is dangerous and will devour any animal or beast that comes in its way. This otter is sometimes described as white with black-rimmed ears and a black cross on its back and sometimes as pure black with a spot of white on its belly. It could only be killed with a silver bullet and the person who killed it would die within twenty-four hours.

It was believed that if you were bitten by an otter, the only cure was to kill and eat another otter. However these days the otter is protected under Irish law and it is a criminal offense to kill one, so you'll have to suffer in silence and get to hospital.

Other superstitions and traditions concerning the otter include the use of the otter as a symbol of a strong family because the otter is a loyal mate and a good parent who will look after its cubs for longer than most other animals. Irish harps used to be carried in bags made from otter skin as it protected them from getting wet. A warrior's shield would be covered in otter skin (lining the inside) and in this way they protected the warrior in battle. It was believed also that the magical power of the otter's skin could be used for healing and it was used to cure fever, smallpox and as an aid in childbirth, while another belief held that if a person licked the liver of a dead otter while it was still warm they would receive the power to heal burns or scalds by licking them.

Many sightings of a king otter have been documented down through the years. Most recently in 2003 when Irish artist Sean Corcoran and his wife claim to have witnessed a *dobhar chú* on Omey Island in Connemara, County Galway. In his description the large dark creature made a haunting screech, could swim fast and had orange, flipper-like feet.

As a matter of interest, the modern Irish word for an otter is '*dobhar chú*', although '*madra uisce*' is also used. The *dobhar chú* may be a relative of the giant otter; these are known to grow to over six feet in length and can weigh up to eighty pounds. They are carnivorous and have been known to attack human adults. They have been recorded swimming at speeds exceeding nine miles an hour. They communicate using a variety of sounds depending on the circumstances; if they sense danger they emit a high, piercing screech to warn their mate. So, fact or fiction? I'll let you decide, but be careful when swimming in Lough Mask.

9

Tír na nÓg:
The Land of
Eternal Youth

The direct translation of 'Tír na nÓg' is 'land of eternal youth'. It refers to a mystical land in Irish mythology where the trees are always in bloom and there is always a bard to sing for you, where the food is always bountiful and the drink is always flowing, and, most importantly, a place where you'll never grow a day older. You may live for blissful eternity in this enchanted land. The most well-known story of Tír na nÓg concerns two young lovers, Oisín, son of Finn and Niamh of the golden hair, who was the daughter of the king of Tír na nÓg. Their story is as follows.

Once upon a time, long, long ago in the west of Ireland, there lived a young man called Oisín. One autumn morning he was out exploring the wild hills with the Fianna, who were the ancient warrior-hunters of Ireland. It was a bright but cold and misty morning. Suddenly from out of the mists they saw a white horse appear and upon its back sat the most beautiful woman that Oisín had ever seen. The sun glistened off her hair and she seemed to be surrounded by a magical glow. The horse and rider came to a stop and the young woman spoke to Oisín and the Fianna. As soon as her eyes met Oisín's, they fell in love. He stepped forward and introduced himself.

'I am Niamh of the golden hair, daughter of the king of Tír na nÓg,' she said in a voice that sounded like the most enchanting music that Oisín had ever heard.

'Come with me to my father's land and there you will never grow old nor feel sorrow. My father has heard wonderful things about the great warrior named Oisín and I have come to take you back with me to the Land of Eternal Youth.'

Oisín hesitated for a moment. He thought of his friends and family and how he would be sad to leave them but his hesitation lasted only a moment for he had fallen under a fairy spell and he cared no more for any earthly thing. He cared only for the love of Niamh of the golden hair. He quickly climbed up onto the white horse. Oisín promised to return shortly and they waved goodbye and rode off into the mist. Oisín was never to see his family or his friends ever again.

When they reached the sea, the white horse ran lightly over the waves and soon they left the green fields and woodlands of Ireland behind. The sun shone and the riders passed into a golden light that caused Oisín to lose all knowledge of where he was. He couldn't tell whether they were still crossing water or whether they were on dry land. Strange sights appeared and disappeared. Oisín saw many strange creatures, some wondrous, some terrifying. He tried to ask Niamh what these visions meant and whether they were real or imagined but Niamh told him to say nothing until they arrived at Tír na nÓg.

Eventually they arrived at the Land of Eternal Youth and it was just as Niamh had promised. It was a land where nobody knew sadness, nobody ever aged and everyone lived forever. Together they spent many happy times together but there was always a piece of Oisín's heart that felt empty. He began to feel lonely and missed his home in Ireland. He wanted to see his friends and family once again. He begged Niamh to let him return to Ireland but she seemed to be reluctant to let him go. She finally agreed and gave him the white horse that had brought him to Tír na nÓg but she warned him that when he reached the land of Erin he must not step down from the horse nor touch the soil of the earthly world for if he did then he could never return to the Land of Eternal Youth.

Oisín set off, crossing the mystic ocean once more. Although Oisín thought that only a few years had passed, it had in fact been three hundred years. You see, time slows down in Tír na nÓg and when he arrived back in his homeland he saw that things had changed. The Fianna no longer hunted the green hills and the grand castle where his family and friends had lived was no longer there. All that remained were crumbling ruins covered in ivy. With a feeling of horror, Oisín thought that he had fallen under some fairy spell that was mocking him with false visions. He threw his arms in the air and shouted the names of his family and friends but there was no reply. He tried once more but all he heard in reply was the sighing of the wind and the faint rustle of the leaves in the trees. With tears in his eyes he turned and rode away, hoping that he would find those he was looking for and that the fairy spell would be broken.

Oisín rode for days but found no sign of his people. He rode east and there he saw a group of men in a field. He rode towards them, hoping to find some answers. Maybe they could tell him where the Fianna had gone. As he approached he saw that the men were trying to move a large rock from the field. When he came nearer,

they all stopped working and gazed at him because to them he looked like a messenger of the fairy folk or an angel from heaven. He was far taller than normal men, he carried a beautiful sword, wore bright and shining armour and the horse he rode seemed to float above the ground, casting a golden light around both itself and its rider. Oisín looked at the men and thought how puny they looked. The size of the rock would have meant nothing to the Fianna. He began to feel great pity for these men. He bent down from his horse, put one hand on the rock and, with a mighty heave, he lifted it from the ground and flung it away from the field. The men started shouting in wonder and applauded, but their shouting changed into cries of terror and dismay when they realised what they had witnessed. They began to run away, knocking each other over in the process.

Unfortunately for Oisín, the girth of his saddle had snapped as he heaved the stone away and he fell to the ground. In that second his horse vanished into a mist that came from nowhere. Oisín rose from the ground. Feeble and staggering, he was no longer the youthful warrior he had been but a man stricken with old age, white-bearded and withered, crippled with arthritis. He let out a cry of horror.

The men who had run away looked back across the field and, seeing what had befallen Oisín, they returned. They found him lying on the ground with his face hidden in his arms. They lifted him up and asked who he was and what had happened to him.

With tears in his eyes Oisín said, 'I was Oisín, son of Finn. Can you tell me where he lives, for I cannot find him?'

The men looked at each other and then at Oisín. One of them said, 'Of what Finn do you speak, for there are many of that name?'

'Finn Mac Cool, captain of the Fianna of Erin,' Oisín replied.

'You're a daft old man and you made us daft thinking you were a young man before,' the man said, 'but we have our wits about us now and we can tell you that Finn Mac Cool and all his generation have been dead for three hundred years. They live now only in songs and stories told. We follow another these days. His name is Patrick and he teaches a different way to live.'

Oisín was left to wander Ireland as a lonely old man. He met Patrick and told him of his family, the Fianna who had disappeared from Ireland hundreds of years ago, the magical land of Tír na nÓg and his love for Niamh. As he ended his story, a great weariness swept over him and he closed his eyes and went to his eternal rest.

Today we still tell the story of Oisín, Niamh and Tír na nÓg. If on a misty autumn morning you see a shimmering white horse dancing in the waves, maybe it's Niamh you're seeing, riding her steed as she searches for her long-lost love – or maybe it's just the crest of a wave. I'll let you decide.

10

SEA MONSTERS
OF THE
FAIRY REALM

Murrisk is a small village on the coast road from Westport to Louisburgh, overlooked by our holy mountain, Croagh Patrick, known locally as 'the Reek'. The name 'Murrisk' originated from either '*muir-riasc*', meaning a marsh by the sea, or '*muir-iasc*', meaning sea monster. Irish folklore and superstition suggest that there are creatures of the fairy realm that inhabit the sea, loughs and rivers of Ireland. They have many different names: some call them the aughiskey, the kelpie, or the selkie. Here in County Mayo we have our fair share of them. They are known as spirits of the dead and are considered to be malevolent creatures. Could it have been the sighting of one of these sea monsters that gave rise to the village's name?

THE AUGHISKEY

An aughiskey is a water horse, a creature of the fairy realm. They are said to inhabit the waters of Ireland and at times will gallop out of the crashing waves to venture inland. If you manage to catch one, they are said to be excellent mounts. However, if they hear or see the sea, they go out of control and charge towards it, galloping straight back into the depths, where they came from, taking their helpless rider with them. It has even been suggested that the aughiskey may be related to the *dobhar chú*.

There have been suggestions that the aughiskey is a shape-shifter and some people claim to have witnessed it taking on the characteristics of a man, except for its ears, which remain horse-like, a sure giveaway. According to Irish legends, the aughiskey lures unsuspecting humans onto its back by appearing to be docile. Once the poor, unsuspecting human has climbed onto the creature's back, it suddenly bolts towards the nearest body of water, where it devours its victim, with the exception of the liver, which for some unknown reason it seems to dislike. 'Why doesn't the rider just jump off?' I hear you ask. Well, the explanation is a simple one: the skin of the aughiskey has adhesive properties, so once you're stuck on its back, there's no escape. An aughiskey is said to have inhabited the depths of Lough Mask in County Mayo and was known to prey on local cattle. It was finally killed by a monk from Tourmakeady.

One of the many folk tales told about the Aughiskey that illustrates its evil nature concerns a young boy called Cooney. A water horse that lived in a lough was captured by one of the Cooney boys, who was told by a local wise woman that if he ever let it see water then it would be the death of him. He kept the horse for years and in all that time he had no problems with it. It was the most faithful horse he ever had. However, one day he rode the horse near the lough and it immediately bolted towards the water, carrying the young boy with it. It entered the lough and killed the boy, tearing him to pieces.

THE KELPIE

The kelpie, like the aughiskey, is a creature of the fairy realm and has inhabited the sea, loughs and waterways of Ireland for thousands of years. Those who claim to have seen one describe it as a powerful-looking horse so beautiful it would take your breath away. It is either black or white and appears as though it has lost its way; however, one clue to its origin is its constantly dripping mane. Even when in human form, they are said to be constantly dripping wet and have seaweed or waterweed in their hair. Some people have said its skin is seal-like, smooth but as cold as the fingers of death when touched.

Kelpies also have the magical ability to be shape-shifters, taking on whatever form suits the occasion, be it human or animal. They can transform into extremely beautiful women or very handsome men in order to lure you into their trap. Some say that when the kelpie takes the form of a human woman, she is often referred to as a water wraith and is most often seen clothed in a green dress. She is just as treacherous as a male kelpie.

There has been a suggestion that it is the nostrils of the horse that create the illusion of perfection. One reason for creating illusions is to keep itself hidden. When it is underwater, only its eyes appear above the water surface, as if searching for its next victim. Like the crocodile, which has a similar habit, you would be very wise to stay well clear of them.

Once again, the ferocious nature of the water horse is apparent. Tales are told of the kelpie luring people to their death. Children are said to be lured into the water, where the kelpie drowns them, rips them to pieces and devours them. It does this by encouraging

Croagh Patrick

innocent children to ride upon its back. Once they climb up onto the kelpie, they become stuck like a fly upon a spider's web for, like the aughiskey, the skin of its back is adhesive. It will then take them into the deep, dark depths of the water and eat them, all except the heart and liver. It's certainly one tale to tell your children to keep them away from the water's edge.

As with all folklore you will find exceptions to the rule and the tale that follows is one example of this.

THE KELPIE WHO FELL IN LOVE

As the magical age came to an end in Ireland and those of the fairy realm prepared to travel to Tír na nÓg, a water horse decided he didn't want to leave the west coast of Ireland. Well, who could blame him? He rose above the waves, came ashore, took on human form and went in search of a wife. However, after attempting to court a local girl who, like most of our women in County Mayo, was very clever, he was not having much luck. The young girl decided to consult a local druid about the situation. The druid realised that the young man was in fact a kelpie and ordered his capture. He was then forced to work in order to learn both humility and compassion and, dare I say, a little bit of honesty. Well, these were not easy lessons for him to learn but eventually the druid decided that the kelpie had indeed learned his lesson and so he was given a choice: he could leave the west of Ireland and go to Tír na nÓg or drink a magic potion that would make him a real man. The kelpie, now deeply in love, decided to drink the potion, which immediately erased all his memories and magical abilities as a kelpie. He and the young girl married and went on to have many children. As far as I know, their descendants still live in County Mayo.

Another story involving a kelpie who took a human wife has less of a happy ending and serves as a warning to anyone who might contemplate marrying a good-looking man who always seems to be wet and has a strange habit of wearing smelly weeds in his hair.

THE KELPIE'S WIFE

There once was a kelpie's wife who lived beneath the lough with her baby son, whom she loved dearly. The kelpie's wife loved her husband but she missed the warmth of the sun and her family, for the kelpie had stolen her away from them without so much as a farewell. One day, when her husband was out hunting for victims, the cold and the darkness became unbearable and she fled to the surface, leaving her baby son behind for she thought the kelpie loved his son and would care for him. Once at the surface, she basked in the warmth of the sun and soon made her way to her parents' cottage. Her family were overjoyed to see her for they thought she had died. In celebration they held a great *ceílí*. The *ceílí* went on late into the night and the kelpie's wife soon forgot her husband and child, overjoyed to be reunited with her family. During the night, there came a great storm and suddenly, from outside the cottage, they could hear the sound of a horse's hooves.

The kelpie had returned to his home beneath the sea and had found his wife gone. He was furious for he loved her so dearly that he viewed her escape as the ultimate crime. Taking the form of a black stallion, he banged on the cottage door but he could not enter for he had not been given permission to cross the threshold. He called for her in rage-filled screams. The kelpie's wife was frightened and also sad, for she loved her husband but wished to stay with her family. During the night, they heard a great 'thud' as something hit the door. After this, there was silence. In the morning, when the kelpie had returned to the lough, they found the decapitated head of the kelpie's son lying on the ground. In revenge for his wife's betrayal he had slain his only son. This was the price to pay for breaking the kelpie's heart. The kelpie's wife lived contentedly and was never again bothered by the kelpie, who had learnt his lesson about love.

They weren't the best of parents.

THE SELKIE

In Irish folklore, there are many stories about creatures who can transform themselves from seals to humans. These particular beings are called selkies, silkies, selchies, roane or simply seal people. The myth of the selkies has all the qualities of a good Irish tale.

During the day, selkies are said to exist as seals, swimming in the cool depths of the sea. At night they come up onto the rocks, shed their skins on the sandy beach and hide them carefully. Having removed their sealskin, they shape-shift into human form. There is no agreement among the stories about how often they can make this transformation. Some say it is every year on Midsummer's Eve, while others say it could be every ninth night. Once ashore, the selkies are said to dance and sing in the moonlight. Although most mythological sea creatures were considered hostile or even evil, selkies were mostly considered to be gentle beings, perhaps because seals have such kind eyes.

Their human selves are beautiful, with dark hair and eyes and a creamy white skin. Real humans are instantly enamoured with them and try to win their love. Selkie women were said to be so beautiful that no man could resist them. They were said to be perfect in every way and made excellent wives. However, the only way a human can keep a selkie is to find their skin and hide it for without their skin they cannot transform back into a seal. The female selkie is said to be a good wife, yet she is solitary and quiet. Legend tells us that children born of a selkie have their dark hair and large dark eyes and an unusual affinity with the sea.

A selkie that is trapped on land will always long for the sea. They will wander the cliffs and beaches, singing sadly about their former home. If a selkie finds its skin, it will return to the sea and never return but if a female selkie has children with a human, she will swim close to their land-based home to keep watch over them and sometimes even play with them in the water, but according to legend 'neither chains of steel nor chains of love can keep her from the sea' and she will always return to the ocean.

The meetings and mating between selkies and humans are usually accidental. However, if a mortal desires a certain selkie there is a ritual that they can perform. At high tide they must wade into the water and shed seven tears into the sea. Then the selkie will come in search of that human. In stories, it is almost always a human man who steals the skin of a female selkie while selkie men are typically seducers of mortal women. Selkie men are very handsome and they take off their sealskins and go looking for 'unsatisfied women', generally women unhappy in their marriage. Usually the selkie males are not willing to stay with them, preferring to return to the sea immediately. However, it has been said that sometimes they take the women with them. These stories may have been used as an explanation for married women who had affairs or ran away from their families. It was also said that if a woman went missing while at sea, it was because her selkie lover had taken her back to their underwater home.

The origin of selkies is lost in the mist of time; however, it has been suggested that they were fallen angels, like the fairies, except that they had fallen into the sea and became seals. Others insist that the selkies were once human beings who, for some grave offense, were doomed to take the form of a seal and live out the rest of their days in the sea. It is also said that selkies were actually the souls of those who had drowned. One night each year these lost souls were permitted to leave the sea and return to their original human form. Others have suggested that when Ireland became Christianised, selkies were used to explain humans in purgatory, caught between two worlds.

Another suggestion for the legend of the seal people was that it accounted for the types of conditions we now recognise as having a medical explanation. Sometimes children were born with seal-like faces, which could have been a rare medical condition called anencephaly, while others had scaly fish-smelling skin, probably resulting from icthyosis. The people of the Orkney Islands say that when a selkie and a human reproduce, all their children have webbed fingers and toes at birth. When this webbing is clipped, to allow handwork, a horny growth appears. These growths could be accounted for by a condition called simple syndactyly and it appears to be hereditary. The selkie legend was probably attributed to these conditions that people could not explain at the time.

In the 1940s and '50s, the people of Ireland and Scotland were surveyed about selkies. When asked if they believed in selkies, it was found that some of the older people, particularly those who had lived their whole lives in isolated villages, believed in the stories told. Some younger people, particularly those who lived on the mainland, admired the stories and saw them as a part of their cultural heritage, but did not believe them to be literally true.

For many people, both in the past and the present, selkies represent a wild, untamed beauty. For a country surrounded by the ocean, inhabited by many people who make their living off it, it is natural that its folklore reflects that beauty. There is a spiritual freedom, mystery and gratification of magically being able to travel between the separate worlds of the sea and the land, which relates to the people's strong dependence on and bond with the unpredictable sea. As the saying goes, 'the sea gives and the sea takes away'. This is best represented in the folklore of the selkies.

There is a folk tale about the dangers of holding a selkie against her will and it is called 'The Selkie Bride'.

THE SELKIE BRIDE

Once upon a time, long, long ago, a fisherman spent all day trying to catch a few fish but those he caught were only small and wouldn't feed the cat, never mind his empty belly. As the sky began to darken, he rowed his little currach back to shore and decided to take his meagre catch back to his lonely cottage. As he walked towards the cottage he heard the sound of singing. It was more beautiful than anything he had ever heard before and he followed the sound.

Hidden behind a ridge of rocks he saw what very few mortals have ever seen: near the water, a group of selkie people were laughing, playing and singing. The fisherman couldn't believe his eyes. The selkies had cast off their skins and had taken on human form so they could play on the shore. Suddenly, one of the selkies saw him and gave a warning cry. They all ran to the sea and quickly dived in. Slipping beneath the crashing waves, they disappeared.

'Holy mother of God, I must be coming down with something for now I'm seeing things,' said the fisherman.

He turned back towards the cottage but once again stopped for something in the back of his mind was nagging him. He turned back to the shore and there he spotted something black and shiny lying on a large rock. He walked over for a closer look and he saw it for what it was: a sealskin.

'No one will ever believe I've seen the selkies unless I show them this,' he said as he leaned over and picked up the skin, which he slung over his shoulder.

As he walked back to his cottage he began to whistle, for he realised that what he had over his shoulder would bring him a small fortune. Suddenly he heard something coming up behind him and, fearing a thief was about to rob him of his prize, he spun around ready to fight. It was no thief; it was the most beautiful young woman he had ever seen. She was crying so hard that he felt his heart melt.

'Beautiful lady,' he said, 'why do you weep?'

She looked into his eyes.

'Kind sir,' she said, choking back tears, 'you have my sealskin. Kindly give it back, for I belong to the selkies and I cannot live under the sea without my skin.'

He stared at her and immediately knew he had fallen in love with her. He also knew that it was highly unlike that he would meet another woman as beautiful as this one.

'I haven't a notion of giving it back,' he thought to himself, 'and I haven't a notion of letting her go either. I'm keeping hold of this one.'

Clutching the sealskin to his chest he said to her, 'Be my wife, for I have fallen madly in love with you and without your sealskin, you'll have to live on land. I promise I'll make you happy.'

'Please sir,' she cried, 'my folk will be so worried. I must go home. Never could I be happy on land.'

He smiled as sweetly as he could, bowed his head and bent down on one knee.

'Now, my dear, my cottage is a very cosy place. I'll keep you warm by the fire and I'll give you all the fresh fish you could ever wish to eat. I promise you will live a happy life on land as my bride.'

The young woman felt helpless without her skin.

'All right,' she said, 'I'll go to your home with you until you will return my skin.'

For many weeks the fisherman kept the sealskin with him for he feared his bride-to-be would steal it and slip away. However, after a while, she began to settle into life on land and when the fisherman saw she was happy, he stuffed the skin inside a crevice in the chimney.

'She'll never find it up there,' he said to himself.

Another month went by, they married and time passed very nicely indeed. They led a happy life. The fisherman was kind and generous. He truly loved his wife and he always worked hard to make her happy. After a while, the selkie woman grew to love her fisherman husband and sometimes she would sing to him. Those nights he was the happiest man in the world. As the years passed, the couple had seven children and the selkie woman loved those boys and girls with all her heart. Most of the time the family was very happy, though every once in a while the children would find their mother on the beach, gazing wistfully out to sea. They would circle her and ask, 'Mother, why do you look so sad?'

She would shake her head and kiss their foreheads.

'Oh, never mind me, I'm only daydreaming,' she told them.

One day the fisherman and the three eldest children went out in their boat to catch fish. The next three walked to the village to buy some bread and milk and the mother and her youngest son stayed home alone. The mother looked out the window and watched the waves crashing on the shore. Suddenly, far off in the distance, she noticed a band of seals playing and barking amongst the rocks. She sighed deeply and her eyes filled with tears.

Her youngest son ran to her side.

'Mother, what's wrong?' he asked. 'Whenever you look out to sea, you grow so sad.'

Without thinking, she turned and said, 'I'm sad because I was born in the sea. It's the home to which I never can return because your father hid my sealskin.'

Now, the boy, like all children in Ireland, had heard tales of the selkie folk, so right away he knew what his mother must be and he ran to the fireplace, reached up and pulled the sealskin from its hiding place. He held it out to his mother.

'How did you find it?' she asked, astonished at the sight of her skin.

'One day I was here alone with father,' said the boy, 'and he took this from its hiding place and stared at it. I knew it was special and now I understand what it is.'

The woman embraced the sealskin and then she reached for her child and embraced him.

'My darling,' she whispered, 'I will always love you.'

Then, clasping sealskin to her heart, she ran outside and down to the sea. She slipped into her skin and dived into the bracing water.

Soon afterwards, as the fisherman and his children were heading home, they rowed past a group of seals. As they passed, the fisherman noticed a sleek young seal gazing at the boat with a strange expression on her face. As they slowly disappeared from sight, he heard that seal cry, a plaintive sound, before disappearing underwater.

When the fisherman arrived home, he learned what had happened and he felt his heart breaking in two, but he understood his son was a loving boy. He was braver and more generous than the fisherman had ever been.

Forever afterwards, the fisherman and the children missed the selkie woman, but knowing she was happy in the world where she belonged gave them a measure of joy. Many an evening, the fisherman could be seen standing on the seashore, looking out to sea as if waiting for his lost love to come home. Maybe he is still there.

11

THE REMARKABLE
STORY OF A SEAL

The following tale appeared in the *Dublin Penny Journal*, Volume 1, No. 18, October 27, 1832:

In the early nineteenth century, a young seal was captured and domesticated in the kitchen of a gentleman whose house was situated on the seashore. Over time it grew bigger and became familiar to the servants of the household. The seal was a gentle, innocent creature and the family grew very attached to it. It responded to its master's voice and the gentleman described it as being like a friendly, playful dog. Every day the seal went out to fish and it frequently brought home a salmon or a turbot to its master. In summer the seal could be found basking in the sun and in winter it would lie in front of the kitchen fire or, if allowed, it would climb into the big oven, where it would fall asleep.

This went on for years until the gentleman's cattle were inflicted with a terrible disease. It was called 'Crappawn', a paralytic affliction that attacked the limbs of cattle. A number of his cattle died and others were badly affected. He tried all the normal medicinal cures to no avail and in desperation he turned to a local wise woman. To his surprise, the wise woman told him that the death of his cattle was due to the fact that the gentleman kept an unclean beast, the seal, in his house. If he wished to rid himself of the Crappawn disease, he must kill the seal. The gentleman, being extremely superstitious, consented to the old woman's proposal and the seal was put aboard a boat and carried out to the waters beyond Clare Island. Once there, the seal was killed and dumped overboard. The boat returned to land and the gentleman and his family retired for the evening.

The next morning one of the servants woke the master of the house and told him that the seal was quietly sleeping downstairs in the kitchen oven. The poor animal had apparently survived his ordeal, returned to his beloved home and crept in through an open window. That day, another cow was reported to be sick and a decision was taken that the seal must be removed for good. A Galway fishing boat was leaving Westport and the gentleman decided he would get rid of the seal himself. Boarding the fishing boat, he would wait until they were many leagues off Boffin, where he would dispose of the seal once and for all. Having carried out the deed, he returned home and a day and a night passed with no sign of the seal returning. However, late on the second night one of the servants was cleaning out the oven fire, getting it ready for the morning, when he heard a gentle scratching sound on the kitchen door. Thinking it must be the house dog she opened the door and in walked the seal looking extremely tired after his unusual sea voyage. Giving a squeal of delight, he waddled over to the glowing embers of the fire, curled up and fell fast asleep.

The servant went straight to his master and woke him to tell him of the seal's unexpected return. The servant told him that although it was unlucky to kill a seal it might be better to deprive the animal of sight and then once again commit its body to the sea. The master of the house consented to this cruel suggestion and the poor seal that had shown nothing but love and affection for the family was robbed of its sight. The following morning the seal, in great agony now, was taken to the waters on the far side of Clare Island and committed to the deep sea for the last time.

The Remarkable Seal.

A week passed and instead of things getting better they started to get far worse. The cattle belonging to the cruel and uncaring gentleman began to die at a faster rate than ever before and the wicked old hag of a wise woman told him that whatever was killing his cattle was beyond her power to control. On the eighth night after the seal had been committed to the waters of the Atlantic Ocean, a great storm began to batter the seashore and the gentleman's house. In the quiet periods of the storm, a wailing sound could be heard outside the door. The servants all believed it was the sound of the banshee coming to warn those within of an impending death and they hid under the blankets of their beds. When the morning dawned, they opened the kitchen door and found the seal lying dead on the doorstep.

The once fine-looking animal that had been happy and well fed was nothing more than a skeleton. Due to its blindness, it was unable to catch any fish, so the poor thing had wasted away with the hunger. It was buried in the sand dunes and from that moment on misfortune plagued the family. The old hag of a wise woman was hanged for murdering the illegitimate offspring of her own daughter, while everything the gentleman held dear collapsed around him. His sheep rotted away from a mysterious illness, his cattle all died, his fields were covered in blight and none of his children grew to maturity. He was to survive through all of this, cursed to see all he loved and cared for taken from him. Eventually he went blind and died a lonely miserable death.

12

GRÁINNE
NÍ MHÁILLE

She is known by many names: Gráinne Mhaol (Bald Grace), Gráinne Ní Mháille (Grace of the Umhalls), Grania, the Dark Lady of Doona, Grace O'Malley and Granuaile (Gran-oo-ale). She was a contemporary of Henry VIII, Elizabeth I, Edmund Spencer, Walter Raleigh and Francis Drake. She was a mother, a pirate and one of the many great women of Ireland. She was born in 1530 in County Mayo into the O'Malley family, the hereditary lords of Umhall, which included Clare Island, Inishturk, Inishbofin, Inishark and Caher.

Gráinne grew up to become a famous and feared pirate, sea trader and clan chieftain. She was the daughter of Owen O'Malley (Eoghan Dubhdara Ó Máille). He was the clan chieftain who controlled the south coast of County Mayo. One of his castles is situated on Clare Island in Clew Bay. As a young child, she always yearned to join her father at sea but he continually discouraged her, saying the sea was no place for a female. According to legend Gráinne decided to disguise herself by cutting off her long hair, dressing as a boy and boarding her father's ship. This earned her the nickname of 'Gráinne Mhaol', 'Bald Grace'. The nickname stuck and she has been known as Gráinne Mhaol ever since.

The O'Malley clan controlled all the area of Clew Bay and expected taxes to be paid to them by all who sailed or fished the sea off the coast of Mayo. They were generally left alone by the English and Anglo-Irish lords; however, under the rule of the Tudor crown this was to change. The O'Malley clan had built a line of castles along the west coast, which allowed them to keep an eye on their vast territory, both on land and sea. The lord who was in nominal control, Mac William Íochtar Bourke (from an Anglo-Irish family), left them alone. By this time the Bourkes had become more Irish then the Irish themselves.

Gráinne Ní Mháille was educated and could speak in Irish, Scottish Gaelic, English, Latin, French and Spanish. At that time, the majority of the Irish population spoke more languages and were better educated than those across the water due to the fact that the Irish were forbidden from speaking Irish and the common person had better access to a basic education. However, as we know, that was all to change.

In 1546 Gráinne was married at a young age to the head of the O'Flaherty Clan, one of the most powerful clans in the west of Ireland. When he was killed in battle, Gráinne became the head of the O'Flahertys. Gráinne later married another powerful Irish chief, Richard Burke, but divorced him after one year under the ancient Brehon Laws. She got to keep his title and Rockfleet Castle near Newport in County Mayo. As England steadily gained control of Ireland, Gráinne came under increasing pressure to relent to the English crown. An expedition from Galway attacked Gráinne in her castle on Clare Island, so Gráinne turned to piracy, blockading the port of Galway and attacking English ships in Galway Bay.

She was to eventually build up a great deal of wealth. This, together with her noble Irish blood, earned her the title 'Pirate Queen' and she was one of the last Irish rulers of the time to defend against English rule in Ireland. Over her lifetime, the English took over most of Ireland piece by piece through a system known as 'Submit and Regrant', by which they either convinced or forced the Irish clan leaders to surrender their lands and titles to the English crown; they would then be given English titles and control of territory once they had sworn allegiance to the English crown. Some chieftains submitted, some rebelled. Gráinne was one of those who refused the English offer.

At fifty-six years of age, Gráinne was captured by Sir Richard Bingham. The ruthless English governor of Connacht had been appointed by the queen to rule over the re-granted territories. Gráinne was apprehended and along with members of her clan, she was imprisoned and scheduled for execution. Determined to die with dignity, Gráinne held her head high as she awaited her execution. At the last minute, Gráinne's son-in-law offered himself as a hostage in exchange for the promise that Gráinne would never return to her rebellious ways. Bingham released Gráinne on this promise but was determined to keep her from power and make her suffer for her insurrection. Over the course of time, Bingham was responsible for taking away her cattle, forcing her into poverty and even plotting the murder of her eldest son, Owen.

During this period of Irish rebellion, the Spanish Armada was waging war against the English along the Irish and Scottish coastlines. It is not known whether Gráinne assisted the English against the Spanish or if she was merely protecting what little she had left, but around 1588, Gráinne slaughtered hundreds of Spaniards on the ship of Don Pedro de Mendoza near the castle on Clare Island in Clew Bay. Even into her late fifties, Gráinne was fierce in battle.

In the early 1590s, Gráinne was still virtually penniless thanks to the constant efforts of Bingham to keep tight controls on her. There was a rather large rebellion brewing and Bingham feared that Gráinne would run to the aid of the rebels against the English. He wrote in a letter during this time that Gráinne was 'a notable traitor and nurse to all rebellions in the province for 40 years'.

Gráinne had written letters to the queen demanding justice, but received no response. In 1593, her son Theobald and her brother Donal-na-Piopa were arrested by Bingham and thrown into prison. This was the final straw that prompted Gráinne to stop writing letters and go to London in person to request their release and ask for the queen's help in regaining the lands and wealth that were

rightfully hers. The two, who were roughly the same age, admired each other and reached a truce.

Gráinne explained, in fluent Latin, that she was not in fact rebellious in her actions but only that she was acting in self-defence, that her rightful inheritance had been withheld and that it should be returned to her. She also asked for the release of her son and brother. If the queen would agree to this then she said she would use all her strength and leadership to defend the queen from her enemies whether on land or sea. Unbelievably the queen agreed. Bingham was forced to release the two captives but in an act of outright defiance he never returned Gráinne's possessions.

There is an interesting story about the meeting of the two queens. It is said that during the meeting, Gráinne sneezed in the presence of the queen and her lords and ladies. A member of the court, in an act of politeness, handed Gráinne an attractive and expensive lace handkerchief. She took the delicate cloth and proceeded to blow her nose loudly then tossed the kerchief into a blazing fireplace. The members of the court were aghast that she would be so rude as to toss an expensive gift into the fire. The queen then scolded her and said that the handkerchief was meant as a gift and should have been put into her pocket. Gráinne replied that the Irish would never put a soiled garment into their pocket and apparently had a higher standard of cleanliness. After a period of uncomfortable silence, during which the members of the court expected the queen to have Gráinne executed for her rude behaviour, laughter broke out, nervous at first and then hysterical. It is said that the queen was amused.

Another tale that gives us a little insight into the life of Gráinne Ní Mhàille. It is said that, when Gráinne Ní Mhàille was returning from a visit to the English queen, she landed at Howth harbour. Gráinne headed to the nearby Howth Castle, intending to dine with Lord Howth and re-stock her ship in preparation for her voyage back to County Mayo. However, when she arrived she found the gates locked against her and her men. This was a clear breach of the rules of Irish hospitality and she was outraged. The young heir to Lord Howth was down at the seashore with his nurse, looking at her ship. Gráinne was so angry at the insult dealt to her by his father that she ordered the child to be taken and put aboard her ship. The young heir was then taken to her castle in Clew Bay, County Mayo. Negotiations took place with Lord Howth who insisted that no insult to Gráinne Ní Mhàille had been intended. He told her that it was customary for the gates to be locked when the family were at dinner.

She refused to release the child back to his father until an agreement was reached that stated in future when the family went to dinner the castle gates would be left open and an extra place would be laid at the table in accordance with the rules of Irish hospitality. Lord Howth agreed and the custom was strictly observed until his death. There is a painting of the abduction of the young heir of the House of St Laurence by Gráinne Ní Mhàille hanging in one of the state apartments of the castle.

Gráinne Ní Mhàille died at Rockfleet Castle in 1603, the same year as Queen Elizabeth. Tradition has it that she is buried on Clare Island at the abbey which bears the O'Malley coat of arms and the motto 'Terra Marique Potens'. A fitting family motto indeed for Gráinne was powerful on land and especially on the sea.

In a man's world, Gráinne Ní Mhàille developed her own power base contrary to Gaelic and English law. She was a woman of singular strength of character and for that became, along with Róisín Dubh and Cathleen Ni Houlihan, a poetic symbol for Ireland.

13

FOLK TALES
OF CONG

THE WHITE TROUT OF CONG

About two miles west of the village of Cong in County Mayo there is a cave known as 'The Pigeon Hole', or 'Poll na gColum' in Irish. A popular destination for tourists and walkers, the cave can be accessed by a steep flight of limestone steps. Once inside the cave, you will be struck by its size and the river running through it, which at times can be mistaken for the cry of the banshee. The walls are covered with bushes and ivy and this is where the pigeons nest, which is what gave the cave its name. In Irish folklore, the Pigeon Hole is the home of 'The White Trout' or 'The Fairy Fish', which avoids bait and evades capture.

The legend of the 'fairy trout' concerns two young lovers who were engaged to be married. One night the young man was ambushed and murdered and his body was thrown into the nearby lake. The young girl was heartbroken because he meant the world to her and she fell into a deep depression, slowly pining away. Eventually she wandered off and was never seen again; some say she was taken by the fairies. Shortly after her disappearance, a white trout appeared in the local lake. People had never seen such an unusual fish and soon rumours began to spread about the fairy fish. In Ireland, the belief in fairies was very strong and superstition was rife, so the fairy fish was given the greatest respect because it wouldn't do to upset the 'little people', as the fairy folk were called.

As the years passed, the people never bothered the trout and it lived quite happily, doing whatever it is that fish do. One day, a soldier heard the story of the white trout and decided to catch and eat it. Eventually he caught the fish and took it back to his house, where he attempted to cook it. He soon realised that this was no ordinary fish; no matter what he did, it just would not cook. He flipped it from side to side and tossed it over and over in the frying pan but to no avail. The soldier wasn't going to be beaten by a fish, so he decided to eat it anyway. He put it onto a plate and just as his knife touched the skin of the fish, it let out a scream, jumped of the plate and fell to the floor.

The White Trout of Cong

The soldier stood, mouth agape, as the fish transformed into a beautiful young women. Holding out her arm, she pointed to where the soldier's knife had cut her skin. She spoke to him and told him that she was waiting for her one true love to return. She demanded that he give up his evil ways and return her to the lake. The soldier was shocked and, shaking with fright, he told the woman that he was very sorry and that he would renounce his wicked ways, but how could he take a beautiful woman back to a lake and just throw her in? The woman then told him that she would transform back into a fish and that he could take her to the underground river within the Pigeon Hole because the river fed the local lake, so no one would see him and he would be safe. She then transformed back into a white trout. The soldier quickly picked her up, ran to the Pigeon Hole and placed her in the river. As soon as she entered the water it turned blood red for a moment as the cut on her skin quickly healed.

It is said that to this day at certain times you may see a white trout swimming in the lake or the river deep within the Pigeon Hole. Look closely and you will see a red mark upon its side. Some people say it's the mark of a knife cut and some say it's where she was burned in the soldier's frying pan. As for the soldier, well, he changed his ways and never ate fish again.

Captain Webb

Two hundred years ago, there was a notorious highwayman in County Mayo called Captain Webb. His real name was Fitzgerald but he was nicknamed Webb due to a physical deformity, which resulted in webbing between his fingers and toes. He came from a noble and highly respected family and had a great deal of influence in the district. However, Captain Webb had some very dark secrets and he is remembered in Irish folklore for his violence, cruelty and evil deeds.

Webb had an unnatural craving for women. Young, old, married or single – they were all fair game and when he tired of them he had a very special place picked out for them. Just west of the village of Cong in County Mayo is a deep water-filled hole that bears the name 'Captain Webb's Hole'. It acquired this name because it was to this deep, dark hole the notorious villain lured a succession of twelve women, where he stripped them before hurling them down into the depths to die.

The number thirteen was to prove unlucky for Captain Webb as fate took its revenge in the shape of a beautiful young woman. The highwayman had held up a carriage by gunpoint, robbed its passengers, shot the horses and kidnapped the young woman who had been returning home with her mother after a night of entertainment given by a high-ranking lord in the locality. Captain Webb was fully aware of the function; as an important nobleman, he would have been invited and would know of others who planned to attend. Armed with this knowledge, he knew that these two women, travelling with no real protection, would be easy prey, dressed as they were in magnificent clothing and wearing their most valuable jewels. He stripped the mother of all her jewels and items of value and he left her lying upon the road. He had other plans for the daughter; he threw a cloak over her, flung her across his horse and galloped off to one of his many hiding places.

He seemed to have a real fancy for her as he gave up all his other favourites and concentrated all his attention on her, even going so far as taking her with him on all his escapades. However, even she could not hold his attention forever and eventually he grew tired of her. He decided that she must go and join her predecessors. The deep black watery hole was about to gain another tenant. He forced her to go out riding with him as usual and when they reached the hole, Captain Webb told her to dismount and remove all her jewellery, gold and rich garments of silk. After all, she wouldn't need them where she was going. Hearing this, she realised his game and said, 'For pity's sake, do not look upon me while I undress for it is not seemly or right to look upon a woman undressing. Turn your back and I shall unclasp my robe and fling it off.'

Captain Webb was a gentleman, even if he was an incredibly evil blackguard, so he did as she asked and turned his back to her.

It was her last request and it was the least he could do. He remained close to the hole though, so he would be ready to throw her in. He was standing there with his back to her when suddenly she jumped up behind him and, placing both hands on his back, she gave an almighty push. Over the edge went Webb, down into the deep, dark, watery grave from which no mortal had ever risen alive. There he was to remain and be tortured by the twelve ghosts of the women he had consigned to their deaths. At last the county was free of him, free from the evil thief, fiend and murderer – and all because of the courage of a young girl for whom the number thirteen proved to be lucky.

Captain McNamara

County Mayo has had its fair share of highwaymen and George McNamara was another who followed this path of dubious employment. He was a man of considerable means, good appearance and was by all accounts the perfect family man. However, once again appearances can be deceiving. Like most young nobles of the day, McNamara spent his time living a life of wild excess and pleasure. He would stop at nothing, no matter how illegal, to satisfy his craving. Eventually he squandered away all his own money and any inheritance he had hoped to receive. He was living by fraud, lies and an insolent contempt for the rights of others. Surprisingly there were those who suggest he was a lovable rogue and he appears to have been a popular figure in local folklore.

McNamara appears to have had the luck of the devil for just at the time when his finances were at their lowest, he was summoned to court to stand trial for fraudulently disposing of land and stock he had no right or title to. The land and stock in question belonged to a wealthy widow who had a beautiful and expensive house in the locality although she was seldom there. She spent most of her time in Paris or Rome with her only son, a young boy who was heir to the property in question. She had returned home just in time for the trial and decided to attend the proceedings, hell-bent on vengeance. She sat in the best seat in the courthouse and listened as McNamara's previous crimes were read out to the court. He was put through the most torturous examination by the prosecution who brought up every evil and cruel practice carried out by McNamara over the years. Strangely, the widow seemed to hear nothing as she gazed at this handsome, splendid young man with his flashing eyes, his long, raven-coloured hair and his magnificent presence, a young man in the prime of his life.

It was if she had been struck by some magic spell. She called over her counsel and ordered the trial to be stopped without any damages claimed. Naturally, after this a warm intimacy grew up between the widow and the captain and in a very short time they were married. It was a perfect match: she had loads of money and he had none, she liked to give him money and he really did enjoy taking it off her. The young boy, heir to the estate, was brought home from boarding school to live with them for, as the captain explained, it was necessary for the boy to learn how to manage the property.

One evening, McNamara set a rope across a lonely part of the road which he knew the boy would pass when riding home. The horse he was on was tripped up and as he stumbled the young boy was thrown to the ground. Late that night, as the boy had still not returned home, the servants and some of the locals were sent out with torches to look for him. He was found lying upon the road where he had fallen; it was obvious to all that he had been dead for some time.

In her grief, the widow gave up the management of her property, estate and money, entrusting it instead to McNamara, who lost no time in making good use of the large sums of money that now fell under his control. It wasn't long before he had resorted to his old lifestyle of extravagant pleasure and lavish living. What his wife, the widow, felt about this was unknown for no one had seen her and McNamara seemed free to carry on with his evil ways and mad orgies. About a year later it was no surprise to anyone when the news came that the 'rich widow woman', as she was still called, had suddenly died of a fit or a stroke. She was found lying dead in her bed one morning and apparently her husband was grief-stricken. It wasn't long before rumours began to spread that a black mark was found round the rich widow's neck and suspicions were aroused but McNamara was so feared that nothing was said against him. However, he couldn't stop the whispers, the sideway looks, or the pointing of fingers.

The captain lost no time in consoling himself in the arms of a young girl, a favourite of his whom he had been seeing long before the death of his wife. They married and lived a life of wild and reckless abandon; that is, until the money ran out. He then decided to join a band of robbers and thieves who threatened and cheated people at fairs and races and he soon became the terror of the county. His mistake, however, was to make enemies of the Big Joyces of Connemara, who swore revenge.

Around this time the captain had acquired a famous mare called Feenish who could outrun any other horse and go without food for days on end. It was said that he taught that horse all sorts of tricks: how to stand on her hind legs, climb through windows and walk upstairs. It wasn't long before the superstitious locals began to suspect supernatural involvement and rumours spread.

It was said that there was an old raven that lived in a big tree near the captain. One day McNamara climbed the tree, stole the raven's eggs and took them home. He boiled them, took them back to the nest and set them back in place. He then hid and watched for what the raven would do. He saw how wise the raven was for she flew off to a nearby mountain where she had hidden a stone of magic. She rubbed the stone over her eggs and the eggs hatched. In time the young ravens became big and strong, flying around just like all the other young ravens.

McNamara saw all of this and resolved to have that stone at any cost. He waited until the raven left her nest unattended and then he stole the stone from the nest. He decided to test it upon himself. Rubbing the stone all over his body he suddenly felt very powerful. He realised he had acquired extremely magical gifts. He had the power to foresee the future and force others to do his will. He could also tell if danger was near and how to avoid his enemies. He decided to rub the stone over his mare and instantly she acquired the same gifts as her master. She could even understand every word spoken to her, no matter who spoke them. McNamara, now armed with all these new powers, became even worse than before. He robbed and plundered widely. No one was safe. The blood of many an innocent victim was now on his hands.

At last the Big Joyces had had enough and they decided to put an end to McNamara and his evil ways. They gathered together all the Joyces of Connemara and gave chase. They pursued McNamara over bog and hill, mountain and stream. It is said that McNamara fell into a bog and his horse lost all four of her shoes. He then made her swim the river at Cong after riding her hard all day and when they emerged on the opposite bank, the horse dropped dead. It would appear that he thought more of that horse than anything else in the whole world for he was stricken with grief and had her buried on an island in Lough Corrib that still bears her name to this day, Innis-Feenish. As soon as he had buried the horse, all his riches and powers disappeared, his children squandered his money and his two sons met with violent deaths. He was a broken man with nothing left except an old grey horse. He rode the horse to Cork, where he boarded a ship to America, never to be heard of again. So ends the story of Captain McNamara, a thief, a gambler and a murderer.

However, as with a lot of folk tales, there is another version of Captain George McNamara's story. This Captain McNamara was born in Dromyn, County Clare to Florence McNamara in 1690 and he was to eventually acquire land and property in Cong (we now know how). He was known as the Robin Hood of the Irish, risking his life to ease the lives of the poor and oppressed peasantry. It was also said that if he heard of an eviction or ill treatment of a tenant he would immediately raid and rob those responsible, distributing the spoils to the needy. He lived near Cong Abbey and purchased it and the accompanying land in 1740. His brother-in-law, who was a Protestant, held the land in trust for McNamara as he was a Catholic and under the penal laws of the time, no Catholic was allowed to own or purchase land of any value. He is buried in the church of the ruined abbey of Cong.

The Battle of Moytura, Cong, County Mayo

There is an Irish legend about an ancient race of people called the Firbolgs, who were here before the Tuatha Dé Danaan and the Milesians. It is said that they were enslaved by the Greeks and suffered by their hands for three hundred years before they were able to escape. The leaders of the escape were five brothers; they led a revolt of 5,000 men, stole some ships and set sail for freedom, eventually landing on the western shores of Ireland. The five brothers – Gann, Genann, Rudraige, Sengann and Slainge – were separated as their ships were battered by heavy seas and they landed at different places.

It is said that the brothers re-formed at the Hill of Tara, where they divided the country up between them. These divisions of land were what we now call the five provinces of Ulster, Munster, Leinster, Mide (Meath) and Connacht. They still survive to this day, although after the Norman invasion two of the original five provinces merged, Mide and Leinster. Ireland prospered under the rule of the Firbolgs. Even though they had been slaves in Greece, they had still been influenced by the Greek political structures, civic administration and technology and they brought these new ideas with them.

They defeated the Comorians who had ruled the land before their arrival and over time they formed a loose alliance with them to fight off other invaders. This period of prosperity was to last for nearly forty years until one day a new wave of invaders appeared on the horizon. The Tuatha Dé Danaan. One night the king of the Firbolgs had a dream in which he saw a great flock of birds flying in from the sea, the king asked his advisor the meaning of the dream. The advisor explained that the dream indicated an invasion by some magical force of great strength. He was to be proved right; a fleet of ships arrived carrying thousands of warriors. When they had landed on the western shores of Connacht, they proceeded to burn their ships, a clear sign of their intent. They set up camp near the mountains and waited. The king of the Firbolgs sent his greatest warrior, Sreang, to speak with them, hoping to find out what they meant to do. The spokesperson of the invaders informed Sreang that they were related to the Firbolgs and that they were called the Tuatha Dé Danaan. They had come from a land far away and their king was Nuadhu. The spokesperson proposed that Ireland should be divided by the two peoples and Sreang returned to Tara to deliver this proposal to his king.

At this time the seat of the high king of Ireland was at Tara in Mide (Meath) and this was where all major decisions were made. The assembled Firbolgs rejected the Tuatha Dé Danaan proposal. However, the Tuatha Dé Danaan were superior in every way and the Firbolgs realised they were staring defeat in the face. They decided to seek a compromise with the leader of the Tuatha Dé Danaan and proposed an honourable solution: a battle of equal forces on the plain of Maigh Tuireadh (Moytura, County Mayo), which might give them a fighting chance of victory. The Firbolgs were defeated and their king was slain, but there had been heavy losses on both sides. The king of the Tuatha Dé Danaan was impressed by the bravery and courage of the Firbolgs and decided he would allow the Firbolgs to continue to rule Connacht while they would rule the other four Provinces. The Firbolgs continued to live in the west of Ireland but their power slowly diminished.

The Battle of Maigh Tuireadh and Hurling

The battle that took place on the plain of Maigh Tuireadh gave birth to many stories and legends, including one about Balor of the Evil Eye and his death at the hands of Lugh the Sun God, who was one of the Tuatha Dé Danaan warriors. However, another one of these legends describes the battle that took place and it is regarded as one of the earliest references to the game of hurling, which was played by the ancient tribes of Ireland in a slightly different way to how it is played today, a version of the game which dates from 1800 BC. It was recorded in the Irish Annals of 1272 BC that the strongest and most skilled warriors of the Tuatha Dé Danaan defeated their rivals, the Firbolgs in a hurling match to the death at the first battle of Maigh Tuireadh in County Mayo. It is said that there were twenty-seven men on each side and when the game was over, the dead were buried together with full honours under a huge cairn. There is no definitive proof that this match ever took place but it makes for a good story.

Hurley was declared a form of military training under the Brehon Laws. It was a punishable crime to deliberately strike another with a hurley. The laws also stated that if a man was killed or injured by a hurley stick, then either he or his family were entitled to lifelong financial assistance. This must be one of the earliest recorded accounts of a military, disability, or widow's pension. There is even a religious reference to hurley: St Colmcille was visiting Tara in the fifth century when he witnessed a Connacht prince using a hurley to strike and kill a young boy. Although St Colmcille tried to intervene, the prince was executed on the spot, such was the anger felt by all who had witnessed his savage act.

Hurley eventually evolved into a sport and was played by teams from different villages. It was used as a way to settle disputes and could have lasted several hours. However, over time it became more organised and was played for its entertainment value. The game we know today is one of the fastest team sports in the world and is the embodiment of the Irish spirit. The game of camogie, which is played by women, is almost identical to the game of hurling and both games continue to be two of the most popular games in Ireland.

14

The Prophet of
Erris and the
Achill Tragedies

Brian Rua O'Cearbháin was born around 1648 and lived in the parish of Kilcommon in the townland of Inver. He is remembered in Irish folklore as the prophet of Erris in County Mayo and his prophesies have been passed down in the oral tradition from generation to generation. It is said the Brian Rua was granted knowledge of the future after showing kindness to a poor widow.

One cold and stormy day an old woman was asked by her landlord for her rent. She couldn't pay so she asked him if he would give her more time. The landlord asked her if anyone could vouch for her.

'Only God your honour,' she answered, to which the landlord replied 'I'll need a better guarantee than your God.'

It is said that Brian Rua was standing nearby, listening to this exchange of words. He took pity on the poor old woman and paid the rent out of his own pocket, saying 'God is good enough for me'. Local folklore tells us that Brian Rua was never to be poor from that day onwards. When he arrived back at his own house, he was taking off his coat when a jewel fell from his sleeve. He picked it up and something strange happened to him. The moment he touched the jewel he was blessed with the gift of prophecy, although some may think it a curse.

One of his prophesies related to carriages on iron wheels with smoke and fire that would come from Achill. The first and last of these trains would carry home the dead.

THE CLEW BAY DISASTER

On 14 June 1894, just before the railway line between Westport and Achill was completed, a group of young people from Achill left their homes to travel to Scotland. It was something done out of necessity as work was scarce in County Mayo, so every year people from all over Ireland would travel to Scotland to work in the fields, picking potatoes. Three hookers carrying passengers from Achill headed off to Westport quay, where the passengers intended to transfer onto a larger vessel that would take them to Glasgow. As the first hooker (the *Victory*) neared Westport quay, the larger ship came into view (the SS *Elm*) and everyone ran to one side of the boat to get a better look at the ship they were to board. There were 126 people aboard (mostly young women). Unfortunately just at that time a sudden wind rose up and the large sail on the boat moved to the same side of the boat that they had all gathered on. The increased weight caused the boat to capsize, throwing all the passengers into the sea. There were a number of smaller boats that went to their aid and a large number of those in the water were saved but on that day thirty-two young people died and the Clew Bay Disaster took its place in the history and folklore of County Mayo. Twenty-eight of the dead were brought home to Achill Sound and buried in Kildownet graveyard.

The last section of railway track was not opened until 13 May 1895 (Mulranny-Achill Sound), although the first train to run on the tracks ran a year earlier, carrying the bodies of the Clew Bay Disaster. The first part of Brian Rua O'Cearbháin's prophecy had come to fruition.

THE KIRKINTILLOCK TRAGEDY

It was the year 1937 and as usual work in Ireland was scarce. On Wednesday 15 September twenty-six young Irish workers, both male and female, many of whom were related, arrived in Kirkintillock, just outside Glasgow, to go potato picking. They were in high spirits as they had been working on farms in the Edinburgh area for the past three months. It was to be their last job; once they completed their work here they would be returning home to Achill and their families with money for Christmas. Once they arrived, they were taken by their employers in two vehicles to the farm. There wasn't much time to rest; it was getting late and they were due to start work early next morning.

Their accommodation was very basic, nothing more than a wooden shed or 'bothy', as it was known, attached to an old four-roomed cottage. The girls were assigned to the cottage and the boys stayed in the wooden shed. One of the rooms in the cottage was given over to the foreman of the group, Mr Patrick Duggan, and his 12-year-old son. In the early hours of the morning of 16 September 1937, tragedy struck. Tommy Duggan, the foreman's son, was unable to sleep and around 1 a.m. he decided to go for a walk. He stepped out of the cottage and was horrified to see that the bothy was on fire. He quickly raised the alarm. Imagine the panic as everyone tried in vain to open the door of the bothy, which had been locked and bolted, and the screams of those inside as they realised they couldn't get out.

Smoke filled the bothy. The straw beds that the boys were sleeping on had caught fire. Those inside clawed at the door and the windows in a desperate effort to escape but to no avail. The young girls from the cottage cried out in horror as they realised the fate of their relatives trapped inside. Eventually one of the owners arrived on the scene with a group of men and they began to fight the fire but it was too late; the shed was engulfed in flames and no sound could be heard from inside. The fire claimed the lives of ten young men and boys between the ages of 13 and 23. They were found huddled together against a wall inside. It was later reported that the local fire brigade had difficulty in identifying those who were in the shed because their companions could only speak Irish. It was suggested that their inability to converse in the English tongue may have been due to the distressed condition they were in.

In the local area, news of the fire and the tragic loss of life shocked the residents but it was nothing compared to the scenes in Achill Sound when news reached the town. Large crowds congregated around the Garda station and the post office as they anxiously waited for news of their children. As news of the deaths spread, weeping mothers fell to their knees in shock and horror.

Two years before the Kirkintilloch disaster, another tragedy had struck the area when nineteen young people had lost their lives when the boat on which they were travelling sank on its way home to Arranmore from Britain. Those nineteen workers had stayed in the same bothy in Kirkintillock on their last working day in Scotland.

The bodies of the ten young men and boys were brought home to Achill Sound amid scenes of heartrending grief. They were laid to rest in Kildownet cemetery, the same cemetery where the victims of the Clew Bay disaster were buried in 1886. Throughout their journey across Ireland huge crowds lined the route to pay their respects to the dead. Crowds in Castlebar and Westport knelt on the platforms of the railway stations. The bodies were brought to Westport and the now disused railway line was re-opened one last time to allow the coffins to be transported by train to Achill for burial. By the time the train reached its final stop there were approximately three thousand rain-soaked mourners to meet it, around half the population of Achill at that time. Two weeks later the line was closed permanently and the track removed, fulfilling the final part of the prophecy of Brian Rua O'Cearbháin.

Today the station and the site on which it stands are in private hands. The railway lines and sleepers have been taken up and sold and the main building has been renovated and turned into the Railway Hostel. The railway line has now become part of the Greenway Trail, which allows people to walk or ride their bicycles in a safe and green environment while enjoying Ireland's beautiful scenery. So from death and tragedy came rebirth and a vision of a better life to come. In many ways it is a fitting tribute to those young people whose lives were taken in those tragic circumstances.

15

THE CÓISTE BODHAR

In Irish folklore the death coach is known as the *cóiste bodhar*, meaning death or silent coach, and if you see or even hear it then either you or a close relative will die in the very near future. The belief is that once the coach has come to the land of the living, it cannot return empty. Once death has come to collect there is nothing on earth you can do to prevent it.

The headless horseman that drives the coach is known as the *dullahan*. He is often accompanied by the banshee, flying along-side the coach wailing and screeching out a warning to certain families that one of their members is about to die. We shall hear more of them later.

The story of the death coach is found in folklore throughout Europe but especially in Ireland. It is a legend that is both widely known and feared. In every country where it is recorded in folk-lore it is treated with fear and respect for it always represents death. It seems that the one thing that unites all people is the fear of the unknown, especially when it comes to death. Why do we still believe in these old tales of superstition and signs of ill omen? Maybe it's because it is still the one thing we have no control over. Yes, we may put it off for a time, but in the end it is inevitable. It is the one

journey that we will all take for, as the old saying goes, 'There are only two things we can say are certain in this life, death and taxes'.

The *cóiste bodhar* is mentioned by W.B. Yeats in his collection *Folk Tales of Ireland* and there are many stories in County Mayo about its appearance. One such tale concerns the activities of a wild and reckless young man in Ballina, County Mayo.

THE BLACK COACH

The ruined Castle Gore in Ballina, situated near the northern end of Lough Conn, is the setting for a macabre tale concerning the fate of a reckless young man, Lord Tirawley. It was reported in *Folk-lore* in 1918. The title Lord Tirawley was borne by just one man, eighteenth-century MP James Cuff, and the legend probably concerns his illegitimate son who scandalised the neighbourhood in the early nineteenth century by keeping a French mistress at Castle Gore.

The story relates how the young man, who was very wild and reckless, was taken from this world. One evening, it is said, just as the nobleman was preparing for a night's partying, a black coach drove up to his door, a stranger asked to see him and, after a long private conversation, drove away as mysteriously as he had come. Whatever words had passed between them, they had a wonderful effect on the young man, who immediately changed his wasteful and drunken ways and proceeded to live the life of a reformed man.

As time went on the effect of whatever awful warning we presume the mysterious visitor had given him wore off and he began to live a life that was even wilder and more reckless than before. On the anniversary of the visit he was anxious and gloomy, but he tried to make light of it. The day passed and at night there was the usual drunken partying going on in the banquet hall. Outside it was wet and stormy. Just before midnight the sound of a carriage was heard in the courtyard. All the noise stopped. The servants opened the door in fear: outside stood a huge dark coach with four black horses. The 'fearful guest' entered and beckoned to Lord Tirawley's illegitimate son, who followed him to a room off the hall. The friends, sobered by fear, saw through the door the stranger drawing a ship on the wall. The piece of wall then detached itself and the ship grew solid. The stranger climbed into it and the young man followed without a struggle. The vessel then sailed away into the night and neither it nor its occupants were ever seen again.

THE DEATH COACH

Here is a story that I have written that reflects the fact that the Death Coach was not always feared. Sometimes it was looked upon as the inevitable last step on the journey through life.

The sound of the church bell can be heard in the distance. It is midnight on a cold winter's evening. The streets of Westport are silent and most people are tucked up safely in their beds after a hard day's work. The night is dark, clouds blocking out the moonlight, and the wind sounds mournful as it rattles the windowpane.

In one of the houses a man sits by the window, waiting patiently for a sign of the doctor approaching. In the bed his dear wife lies silent. By the flickering light of the fire he can see her face, older now but still as beautiful as she was the first day he saw her at the village dance all those years ago. She looks drawn and every so often her face wrinkles as if in pain. The medicines don't seem to work as they used to and it upsets him to see her so. He walks over to the bedside and strokes her brow. She holds his hand tightly and he can feel the coldness of her skin. Her breathing is shallow and quick now and he knows in his heart and soul that she is slowly drifting away. In one way he is happy for her as it means she will be free from pain but for this he feels guilty. He cannot bear to see her in so much pain. Sometimes she looks as if she wants to scream out in desperation, 'Don't leave me', and yet he knows he must for he cannot go with her on this journey – not tonight, not yet.

He hears the sound of horse's hooves and the clatter of wheels rolling over the cobbles. He gently frees his hand from hers and walks over to the window, expecting to see the doctor arriving. It's not the doctor's carriage he sees outside but a black coach that has no horses and yet he can still hear the sounds of hooves and heavy breathing even though the shafts are empty. The doors of the coach are closed; there are black holes where there should be windows. Slowly the coach approaches.

He breathes out a heavy sigh and is filled with deep sorrow for he knows it is the death coach. His wife had said that it would come for her tonight but he had told her not to be silly, she would soon be up and about, wasn't the doctor coming and he'd give her some medicine. He didn't believe in such nonsense. He didn't want to believe. However, his eyes tell him now what his heart knew to be true for it stops outside and the door slowly opens. His heart thumps in his chest as he takes in the terrible sight. He walks over to the bed, clutches his wife's hand once again and she opens her eyes and smiles that gentle smile he knows so well. She tries to squeeze his hand in return but she is too weak.

'Is it here?' she asks, her voice a bare whisper.

He nods.

'I love you so much,' he says to his wife as he leans down and kisses her. As he does so he can feel her last breath on his lips. It is as if her very soul has passed through him. Her grip loosens and her hand gently falls away. She has gone from this world and he knows she has died. He stands up straight and looks upon her face with great tenderness and love, the tears flowing silently down his cheeks.

'Goodbye, my love.'

As he stands there, not knowing what to do, he sees a movement out of the corner of his eye. He looks over and sees his wife standing by the door. He looks back to the bed and sees the body of his wife lying there, looking for all the world as though she is asleep. He looks back at what he now believes to be his wife's spirit; she smiles at him, turns and walks through the door. He hurries over to the window and looks out, hoping to see her just once more. He sees her walk over to the open door of the coach. Pausing for a second, she looks towards the window; it's as if she knows he is standing there. She raises her hand and gives one last gentle wave. He waves back, his heart breaking, tears streaming down his face. She turns back and steps into the coach and the door closes behind her. The horseman raises his whip and the coach slowly moves away and then is gone.

'Goodbye my love,' he calls gently. In a way he knows her pain is over but for him it has just begun and with a heavy heart he turns away. Hearing a knock at the door, he opens it to find the doctor standing there.

'Hello, doctor, she's dead,' he says, and the tears flow once again.

The Dullahan

'The *Dullahan* serves no master but death.'

The Irish *dullahan* (also *Gan Ceann,* meaning 'without head') is usually seen either driving the death coach, which is pulled by six black horses, or riding alongside on a black stallion, which may also be headless. He is a soul collector who roams the country-side around midnight on certain Irish festive days. He dresses in a long black cloak and is usually seen riding the black horse with his decapitated head under one arm. The head's eyes are massive and constantly dart about like flies while the mouth is always in a hideous grin that touches both sides of the head. In some of the stories his horse has a head which is longer than its body by six yards and has flaming eyes and short ears.

The flesh of the *dullahan*'s head is said to have the smell, colour and consistency of mouldy cheese. He has a large mouth filled with razor sharp teeth, filed to a point. The *dullahan* whip is actually the spinal column of a human corpse and the wagons they sometimes accompany are also decorated with the remains of corpses. Human skulls take the place of candleholders and the cover of the coach is usually made from the shroud from a coffin. When the coach reaches the abode of the person picked by death, the *dullahan* calls out their name and they immediately die.

There is no way to bar the road against a *dullahan*. All locks and gates open on their own when it approaches. *Dullahans* do not appreciate being watched while on their errands, throwing a basin of blood on those who dare to do so (often a mark that they are among the next to die) or even lashing out the watchers' eyes with their whips. Nonetheless, they are frightened of gold and even a single gold pin can drive a *dullahan* away.

It was once believed that the *dullahan* was sent by the queen of the fairies to punish mortals that had betrayed the secrets of the fairy folk. He would visit you as you slept and one touch of his hand would cause the muscles of your arm or leg to wither and die. He would then leave as silently as he came.

Some people believe that the *dullahan* is the embodied spirit of a Celtic god, Crom Dubh, who demanded human sacrifices each year. The worship of Crom Dubh continued in Ireland until the sixth century when Christian missionaries arrived from Scotland. However, Crom Dubh, still wanting souls, became the *dullahan* or the *fear dorcha* (which translates as 'dark man').

In some legends the *dullahan* and the banshee are said to join forces. The *dullahan* and the banshee (*bean sidhe*), are members of the Unseelie Court, which consists of all the bad or evil fairies, as opposed to the Seelie Court, which is made up of the good fairies. Those members of the Unseelie Court who fly through the night are called The Host or The Horde. It was said that any mortal unlucky enough to cross paths with The Host would be attacked and forced to participate in their nocturnal activities. It has been suggested that the early Christian Church invented these stories to stop pagans from leaving their homes at night and participating in fertility rites at Bealtaine and other important rituals at other times of the year (Samhain, etc.).

> Faeries come take me out of this dull world,
> For I would ride with you upon the wind,
> Run on top of the dishevelled tide,
> And dance upon the mountains like a flame.
>
> (W.B. Yeats, *The Land of Heart's Desire*)

THE BANSHEE

When most people mention a banshee, they do so in the context of a harbinger of death. However, according to Irish folklore the banshee's true role is that of a protector or guardian angel-type spirit. She will appear shortly before a death occurs in one of the families she guards. I describe it as a 'she' for the banshee is traditionally female in appearance.

Depending on the observer, the banshee can appear in many different guises. Sometimes she is young and beautiful, sometimes old and scary. One person may describe her as tall and thin while another will describe her as very small and old.

The legend of the banshee may have originated from goddess known as the Morrigan in Irish mythology. Morrigan is said to appear before a battle. Also described as the 'washer at the ford', she was said to appear as a young woman who washes the blood-stained clothes or the shrouds of those who would lose their lives in the upcoming battle. She was also said to also appear in a variety of other forms, such as that of a hooded crow flying over the field of battle, a stoat, a hare, or a weasel – in fact most animals associated in Ireland with witchcraft.

Also known as the White Lady of Sorrow and the Lady of Death, it is not known when the banshee first appeared but the earliest records that mention her date from the early eighth century.

On occasion banshees have appeared in human form and there are several records of human banshees or prophetesses attending the great houses of Ireland and the courts of local Irish kings. In 1437, King James I of Scotland was approached by an Irish seer or banshee who foretold his murder at the instigation of the Earl of Atholl.

Traditionally, however, the banshee is described as a keening woman. She is said to follow certain old Irish families and will appear before a death and wail and scream. She will be heard by members of the family and may also be heard by others in the area. Sometimes she attends the funerals of the beloved dead and, although unseen, can be heard wailing, her voice blending in with the mournful cries of others.

Although the banshee is said to usually follow those Irish families that have an 'O' or a 'Mac' prefix, this is not always the case as there have been many references to banshees appearing before deaths in certain Anglo-Norman or Anglo-Irish families. It has been suggested that a banshee will even follow a family that emigrates and reference has been made to Irish families whose descendants in countries such as America or Australia have been visited by a banshee.

One incident occurred in 1938 when the Giant's Grave in County Limerick was excavated and the bones taken to a nearby castle. It was said that those who heard the wailing of the banshee described it as if 'every banshee in Ireland was keening'. This may not be that unusual as there have also been reports of large numbers of banshees forecasting the death of major religious or political figures.

The banshee's wail seems to differ throughout Ireland. In some parts of Leinster it is referred to as so piercing that it shatters glass. In Kerry the keen is experienced as a low, pleasant singing, in Tyrone as the sound of two boards being struck together, and on Rathlin Island as a thin, screeching sound somewhere between the wail of a woman and the moan of an owl.

One explanation of the believe in banshees suggests that it derives from the Church's dislike of the Irish tradition of women singing a lament to mourn the passing of a family member, often referred to as keening. To discourage the practice the Church said that, as punishment, keener's were turned into banshees by God.

Another common explanation for the superstitious legend is the cry of the barn owl. In ancient battles, owls would screech and take flight if they noticed an army approaching, which would forewarn the defending army. And it is this screech that became associated with the banshee story.

16

SACRED WELLS

Since time immemorial, Irish people have firmly believed in the healing powers of sacred well waters. Special days were set aside to visit wells and leave gifts in appreciation. The wells were cleaned and generally cared for while the water channels were kept clear to ensure the flow of water in and out of the well's basin. Carrying healing powers and blessings, the water flowed into the nearby streams, rivers and lakes. In this way all life forms dependent on water could benefit.

Here in Ireland we are able to visit holy or sacred wells and witness rituals that have been practiced for thousands of years. In times past a sacrifice was offered up whereas today you might see someone looking to the well for inspiration or good luck. People may drink the waters or wash themselves with it, hoping to cure some illness. In fact the water of some holy wells has been found to contain curative properties, mostly due to the presence of certain minerals. However, the healing influence of the wells was said to be due to more than their medicinal qualities. The well itself was viewed as a shrine, dedicated to the miraculous emergence of living water, in all cultures a symbol of regeneration, purification and the source of life itself. There is still a strong instinct even today when standing near a well or on a bridge over a stream or river to toss a coin into the depths. I think most of us at one time or another have made an offering to the wishing well.

People still make pilgrimages to the holy wells to seek relief for a variety of ills, from rheumatism to scurvy, broken bones to leprosy. The link between water and fertility led to a number of wells gaining a reputation for curing childlessness. Frequently a tree with magical properties – ash, rowan or hazel – was planted beside the well to serve as its guardian. Hundreds of years later, the trees now tower over the water. Petitioners would leave a token piece of clothing, usually hanging on a branch of the tree, so that the healing power of the well could act upon it. Other people would leave pieces of cloth tied to a branch. These pieces of cloth were known as rag cloths and represented some illness or disease suffered by the petitioner. As the rag rotted away and eventually disappeared, so would the ailment.

Dreaming at holy wells was also used as a method of foretelling the future, which is possibly an echo of pagan times when, it seems, a female oracle presided over the well. This ancient practice was preserved down the years, albeit in a humbler manner, by the custom of country girls who would seek to know their future husband at the well.

In Ireland, pilgrimages to holy wells are still an important part of the year and a high number of these fall upon the Celtic festivals of Imbolc on 1 February, Bealtaine on 1 May, Lughnasadh on 1 August and Samhain on 1 November. These are all special turning points of the year when the gates of the other world are opened. Numerous holy wells are in fact dedicated to the Celtic goddess, Brigid, and you will find that many contain variants of her name. A ritual practice dating from prehistoric times and continuing to this day is that of circumambulation, or making structured rounds of the well, always in a clockwise direction (*deiseal*).

Christianity did not alter the people's belief that the wells had healing powers. The great nineteenth-century Irish playwright J.M. Synge, while living on the Aran Islands, wrote *Well of the Saints*, a comedy based on accounts of miracles that occurred at

Tobar an Ceathrar Álainn (Well of the Beautiful Saints), which is found on Inishmor, just a few metres from a church dedicated to Saints Fursey, Brendan, Conal and Bearchan. In the play, Martin and Mary Doul, a blind beggar couple, believe themselves to be beautiful until a friar restores their sight with water from a holy well. No longer disabled, they discover they are not only common-looking but now have to work for a living. When they become blind again and the friar attempts to restore their sight a second time, Martin knocks the holy well water to the ground, choosing blindness and a beggar's life, having 'seen' enough human cruelty.

SACRED WELLS IN COUNTY MAYO

'*Tobar*' is the Irish word for a well and you will find the word as part of many Irish place names dotted around the country, such as Tubberclare (Tobar Chláir), meaning 'well of the plain', or Tobercurry (Tobar an Choire), meaning 'well of the pot'. There are hundreds of sacred or holy wells in County Mayo and it is not my intention to name them all. However, the holy well in Ballintubber (Baile an Tobair), from which the town gets its name ('village of the well'), has been famous for hundreds of years. It was said that a great healer lived beneath the rock from which the water flowed and the well was worshipped by the local people who called it the 'King of Waters'. St Patrick is said to have uncovered the well to show that there was nothing beneath it. He then blessed the well and baptised one of his followers in its waters. The name of this disciple was Cainnech and Patrick placed him in charge of the local church of Cell Tog.

There are numerous wells dotted around Ireland which bear St Patrick's or St Brigid's name as it was normal practice to dedicate sacred sites or wells to the memory of particular saints. Churches will also be found in the vicinity of sacred wells due to the fact that these sites were already traditional sites of ritual and water was necessary for both the needs of the holy men and women who lived there as well as for baptism. The references to holy fish or fairy fish found in sacred wells may also be connected to the fact that some of these followers of the 'new religion' may have kept fish in these wells for their own use. No one would interfere with these fish as it would be viewed as a serious crime to rob a holy man of what little he had, so the fish would also have been considered blessed.

In Aughagower, County Mayo, St Patrick founded a church for his disciple Senach. Patrick loved the village so much he wanted to stay there but he was refused permission by an angel as God had other plans for the saint. Patrick then decided to place two salmon in the local river for Senach's use. The fish are said to have always remained together and they could not be harmed because Patrick left the angel to watch over them. They may still be there today which is more than can be said for the holy well. That disappeared due to a modern drainage scheme.

There is a stained-glass window in the Coill Míolcon church in the Maam Valley and although this is quite a distance from Inishglora it commemorates a miracle performed by St Brendan the Navigator. It depicts St Brendan with a woman and child. It is said that the child was the last heir of the O'Malley clan and was extremely sick. The woman was the mother of the child and she had been advised to take the child to St Brendan on Inishglora where he had founded a monastery. St Brendan immersed the child in the water of the holy well and he was immediately cured. The child grew up to become the clan chieftain, led the O'Malleys on land and sea and actually saved the clan from extinction. The window is the work of Evie Hone and was commissioned by a local O'Malley family. The holy well on Inishglora is called *Deirbhile* in the native tongue of the islanders.

Thomas Johnson Westropp mentioned the well in his archaeological survey of Clare Island's Holy Monuments, published 1911-1915. He worked under the supervision of Robert Lloyd Praeger. He referred to the well as 'Tobar Féile Bhrid', which translates to 'Well of the Festival of Bridget'. This well would appear to still be a site of pilgrimage and it has been suggested that it has connections with a number of cures: a young boy with a limp who slept next to the well as his mother said her prayers and an older man from Ballinrobe who was said to be an invalid. They spent a week on the island, drinking water from the well and performing ritual prayers. Both of them were to recover from their ailments; the boy was cured of his limp and the man had his health restored.

Gráinne Ní Mháille (Grace O'Malley) also has a connection to Tober Feile Bhrid. It is said that she married a shipwrecked sailor at the altar near the well. His name was Hugh de Lacy and he was fifteen years younger than her. He was the shipwrecked son of a Wexford merchant whom Ní Mháille had rescued. Unfortunately her new husband was later killed by the MacMahons of Ballycroy, who had a curse put on them for killing another man on Achill Island. Gráinne heard the MacMahons were making a pilgrimage to Caher Island to purge the curse; she ordered her galleys to set sail and hid behind the island. When the MacMahons landed she sprang her trap and captured her husband's killer. She took him back to Clare Island where she hanged him. As with other holy or sacred wells, Tober Feile Bhrid is said to contain a holy fish, a trout that is seen by only the most devout.

17

THE LOVE FAIRIES

THE LEANNÁN SIDHE

The *leannán sidhe* is known throughout the Celtic world. The name means 'fairy of inspiration' and legend tells us that the *leannán sidhe* lives under the Irish Sea. It is said that the *leannán sidhe* is a dark fairy, evil and dangerous and appearing as incredibly beauty to mortals – so beautiful in fact that all other mortals become dull and lifeless when compared to it. W.B. Yeats put the *leannán sidhe* into the same group as witches and malevolent spirits.

Only one *leannán sidhe* exists and she is more a force than a woman. The translation of her name holds the first clue to whom and what she is. The words are Gaelic and refer to a fairy muse. '*Leannán*' means 'the love of my soul or spirit' or even 'my inspiration' while '*sidhe*' is the word for a fairy. *Leannán sidhe* is often quoted as meaning 'the fairy mistress' or 'the fairy sweetheart'. She is the famous Celtic muse with such a dark and unearthly beauty that her lover was often distraught with longing and suffering in her absence. She is a fairy mistress of dreadful power for she seeks the love and dominion of mortal men. If they refuse her, she becomes their slave and if they consent, they become hers. Most men find that they cannot refuse her.

No one has ever described the *leannán sidhe*. Perhaps each stricken man jealously guards his love and fears the world's knowledge of her. However, it is more likely no mortal can describe her because she is pure desire itself and she will avoid every effort to limit her powers. She may select her lovers from our realm, but she never allows her story to remain long on their mortal lips. The memory of her is like a passing mist, impossible to grasp or to hold.

She does not play with emotions; all who love her live for her and their desire for her frequently destroys them. To be in the arms of the *leannán sidhe* is to be ensnared by a dominatrix. The more suffering she inflicts, the dearer she becomes to them. The more they desire her, the more she slips through their fingers. Her absence is like a chain pulling them towards her. An impatient mistress, the *leannán sidhe* creates such desire in her lovers that they will overcome all obstacles to embrace her. She never yields to them in mortal lands, but insists on their meeting in Tír na nÓg so that men must pass through death to enjoy her.

W.B. Yeats suggested that the *leannán sidhe* was similar to a blood-sucking vampire, which may at first seem a little dramatic but it fitted into the Victorian idea of the Christian superstition of the succubi. The succubi were believed to be extremely beautiful females of supernatural origin who seduced and enchanted men. Unfortunately there appear to be very few written accounts of the *leannán sidhe* prior to W.B. Yeats. However, there is a rich cache of folklore that concerns the *leannán sidhe* and the love fairies, which is far more interesting than the popular vampire myth.

In Irish folklore the *leannán sidhe* is a muse of poetry or music and often takes an artist for a lover. It is said that her lover gives her the vital depth of emotion that she craves and she in turn inspires his genius, giving him the ability to create a work of art, music, or poetry with great depth of feeling. Her true purpose is revealed in the creative works she inspires in poets, painters and musicians. She is an empath who is compelled to inspire love and despair, longing and desire. She teaches the beauty and power of such emotion as well as teaching that all such feeling is vital to creation, with many dark nights of the soul required to convey the sorrow of her history. She has an otherworldly sadness and regret for the glorious past of the Irish, something that still resonates through Irish music and poetry up to this day. She is intelligence and creativity, art and magic.

The price of her gift is often a sorrow or heartbreak that is born of obsession. It has even been said that she gives the gift of creativity in exchange for the artist's life. Without her inspiration the artist is lost, unable to create or compose. He will often fall into a state of deep depression. Sometimes he will commit suicide or just give up his creativity and slowly fade away. However, the artist who loses his gift of creativity has in many ways spurned the love of the *leannán sidhe* but unfortunately he will never understand the connection between the two. When the nature of the *leannán sidhe* is understood then it will shine as a beacon, lighting up the darkness.

It is said that those who devote themselves to the *leannán sidhe* will live a short but glorious lives. However, to be fair, it may be the destructive nature of the artist that has given rise to the description of the *leannán sidhe* as evil and dangerous. Musicians, artists, writers and poets often tend to burn the candle at both ends; they burn brightly but can expire quickly.

History is full of talented artists who died young. There is an urban legend today that has become known as 'The 27 Club'. Some people consider the first member of this club to have been the great bluesman Robert Johnson. Other 'members' of this club are said to be Brian Jones, Jimi Hendrix, Janis Joplin, Jim Morrison, Kurt Cobain and, more recently, Amy Winehouse. All died at the age of 27. However, there are many other arists who also died tragically young, such as Phil Lynott (37), James Dean (24), John Keats (25), Percy Shelley (20), Thomas

Chatterton (17), Christopher Marlowe (29), George Gordon Byron (36) and Robert Burns (37) to name but a few. Their deaths may have been caused by tragic accidents, deliberate acts of self-destruction, or even natural causes. One thing they all had in common was that they were all brilliant and all died young.

The *leannán sidhe* is an empath that inspires love, despair, longing and desire through which we are taught the beauty and power of emotion. However, there is also a dark side to human emotion which conveys the sorrow felt in the soul and the heart. Could it have been this dark side that was considered dangerous and mysterious? She is not evil as we understand evil but she can be dangerous and destructive. If you really understand her true nature, if you do not fear or grovel to her, she will give you all you desire. Whatever you think of the *leannán sidhe*, whether you regard it as something to be feared or something to be embraced, once captured by one you live only in order to please, your own passion leading to your eventual destruction.

DEARG-DUE

Once there was a fair maiden named Dearg-due who was so beautiful that she was known throughout the country. She could have married any man she wanted but she fell in love with a local peasant. This was unacceptable to her father, who forced her into an arranged marriage with a wealthy man to secure the financial future of his family. This new husband treated Dearg-due very badly and she eventually committed suicide, although some say it was a broken heart that killed her.

Her burial was a simple affair. She was buried in a small churchyard, supposedly located near Strongbow's Tree in the village of Waterford. The only one to mourn her death was the young peasant boy who visited her grave every day, tearfully praying for her to return to him. The story tells that a year after her death she rose from her grave filled with vengeance, went to the house of her father and, finding him asleep, placed her lips over his and sucked the life force out of him. She then went to the house of her husband and in a frenzied attack she not only sucked the breath of life out of him but also his blood. It is said that the surge of blood rushing through her body made her feel alive once more.

It is believed that Dearg-due rises from the grave to seduce men and lure them to their deaths by draining their blood. She is always in the form of a beautiful woman. Legend differs on how often she rises from the grave: some say she returns with every full moon, others a few times a year, while others say she rises but once a year, on the anniversary of her death. Most versions of the Dearg-due story claim that she can transform into a bat-like creature, although some versions make no mention of shape-shifting. Some legends say she does not drink blood but sucks out the life force from men until they slowly wither and die. All thoughts of her young peasant boy are long forgotten and of him we hear no more.

According to the legend, the only way to defeat Dearg-due is to pile stones on her grave. While this will not 'kill' her, it will prevent her from rising, holding her at bay. But if the stone pile is not maintained and regularly added to she can escape and is free to roam the night again.

Some people think that Bram Stoker's *Dracula* is based on the Dearg-due. They argue that Stoker had never travelled to Eastern Europe, so he would only know the beliefs of people in those areas from travellers. They go on to say that *Dracula* was written during Ireland's great 'Celtic Revival'. I do not say that what they believe is true, I simply point that there are a number of people who speculate that *Droch fhola* influenced Stoker and that the name Dracula may have its roots in this word. *Droch fhola* was said to refer to the evil eye and its hypnotic influence upon its victim and the use of the 'hypnotic stare' by Dracula is also pointed out. As I say, it may not be true, but there are those who believe it to be. The association with Vlad the Impaler is one suggested derivation of the name *Dracula* but not necessarily the only one.

The Dún Dreach-Fhoula or the Castle of the Blood Visage is supposed to be a fortress guarding the pass in MacGillycuddy's Reeks in County Kerry. The fortress is believed to be inhabited by blood-drinking fairies, although it has never been found and even the locals do not know of its location – or if they do they are not telling.

On the other side of the argument are Irish mythologists who say that the recorded Celtic stories bear no mention of the Dearg-due at all. However, they can't explain the persistence of the oral stories of this Irish vampire. I'll leave you to decide.

THE GANCONER OR GANCANAGH

In Connacht the word is pronounced 'gánconâgh'. The name *ganconagh* comes from the Irish term '*gean cánach*', which means 'love talker'. Watch out for him because it definitely means bad luck is on the way if you meet him. He is a real loner, a solitary fairy who is the embodiment of love and idleness. He always has a dudeen (pipe) in his mouth, although he will never have it lit as fairies hate and despise smoke so an unlit pipe in a lazy man's mouth is always a clue. He is lazy and you would often find him with his hands in both pockets, a purse in one of them, hanging around, watching and waiting.

He has no shadow and when he is around the birds stop singing and a mist unfurls about him. He haunts lonely valleys, speaking his love to milkmaids and shepherdesses, and when he has had his wicked way with them he abandons them (how many times have we heard that story?). They then pine away and even die of a broken heart. In fact it has been said that the *ganconagh* thrives on the sorrow that he leaves behind. This seduction of young maidens seems to be his favourite pastime. Of course, they blame his dark twinkling Irish eyes, his enchanting voice and his pure charm. Whoever had been ruined by ill-judged love was said to have been with the *ganconagh* and men who lost all their money by buying baubles for their ladies were said to have met the *ganconagh*. I think we've heard all that before as well.

The *ganconagh* has been skulking around County Mayo for hundreds of years, usually dressed in the fine clothes of a gentleman. However, he is no gentleman. He will stalk a young female, watching her and listening to her as she talks to others. He will discover her weaknesses and deepest desires and then he will make his presence known. Dressed in his finery, he will seem to satisfy every desire the young girl has secretly harboured, the very sight of him will make her heart miss a beat, his smell will intoxicate her and she will want no other. This is when the *ganconagh* will pounce. As soon as she feels his touch on her skin she is inexplicably addicted to him and will obey his every command.

Once the young girl has been caught in his trap you can be sure that whatever standing she may have had will be destroyed as he will use her and debase her. No matter how pure or virtuous she had been, she will slowly descend to the depths of depravity until her freedom of will and good name are gone forever. She will be disowned by her family, friends and neighbours and driven to deep despair and yet she will be unable to resist. It is this torment that the *ganconagh* feeds on. He will boast of his exploits and will be delighted if he can goad other young men to follow his example by bragging to them, encouraging them to engage in similar behaviour. When the *ganconagh* has grown tired of his latest conquest he will toss her aside and disappear in search of new blood. She will be left heartbroken and lost. She will search frantically for her lost love but to no avail. Eventually she will go mad, fall into a pit of deep despair and lose interest in life itself before finally dying of a broken heart.

You may think that the *ganconagh* that existed hundreds of years ago was just a figment of the imagination or a myth. However, the modern ganconagh may be found in nightclubs, wine bars and hotel lobbies.

One final note: as previously stated the *ganconagh* was often seen with a clay pipe in his mouth and could be recognised by the fact that it was never lit. However, the smoking that now exists in Ireland means you cannot rely on this means of identification. So my advice is:

Beware the tunes that touch your heart.
The gánconágh will play the soul
Beware sweet lass don't crave his art
He'll pierce your heart and leave a hole.

(Anon.)

18

PATRICK AND CROAGH PATRICK

Legend has it that St Patrick fasted on the summit of Croagh Patrick, a mountain in County Mayo known locally as 'the Reek'. It is said that it was upon this summit that Patrick spent forty days and nights in prayer and meditation. It is also said to be from this place that he banished all the snakes and demons from Ireland or, to put it more poetically, 'charmed them into the sea'. Perhaps the snakes Patrick charmed were sea serpents? However, I doubt that they were snakes in any real sense because there haven't been snakes in Ireland since the end of the last glacial period. It has been suggested that the whole legend is really symbolic of St Patrick converting the natives to Christianity and banishing the druids whose symbol was the serpent and who are said to have worn serpents' eggs as amulets. Although banishing the snakes makes for a far better story. It has also been suggested that in the Gospel of Matthew, 'serpent' in Old Arabic means 'wise ones', which would account for Patrick's attempted banishment of the druid class. (As a matter of interest, 'forty' was also a way of saying 'many' in Old Arabic.)

Patrick would have been disgusted by the folk beliefs of the Irish and would have tried to banish such ideas from Ireland. The Irish of that time believed in many different spirits and deities that lived in nature – in the mountains, trees, woodlands and water – and they had a great number of sacred sites that were used for rituals and worship. Ireland carried out trade and exchanged ideas with their trading partners and serpent-worship and serpent symbolism was found right across Europe so it's not surprising that there was a common link between pagan societies. The symbol of the serpent can be found in Celtic artwork in both pre-Christian and Christian Ireland and it is evident on monuments, crosses and illuminated manuscripts such as the Book of Kells.

If, as some have speculated, the Tuatha Dé Danann, the kingly mythological Irish pre-Christian race, were descended from the Israelite Tribe of Dan, then the serpent would have been associated with the people of Danann. The Israelite Tribe of Dan used the serpent to symbolise their tribe from ancient times. In Ireland the snake symbol was associated with some Celtic goddesses and also with the cult of Crom Cruaich. It has been suggested that Crom Cruaich followers demanded human sacrifice to a serpent deity but there is absolutely no evidence to substantiate this claim. This could have been another invention of either Patrick or Julius Caesar or both? Crom Cruaich (Lord of The Mound) was the most ancient and venerated god of all the various tribes of Ireland. Crom Cruaich was said to live in high places, including Croagh Patrick in County Mayo.

It was during his time in Mayo that Patrick was tormented by demons who assumed the shape of black birds. He rang his bell so hard that it could be heard all over Ireland and finally he threw the bell with such force at the demons that it broke and all the birds disappeared. Patrick began to cry and an angel came to comfort him. The story goes that he asked the angel to intercede on behalf of the Irish people to gain special dispensation for them on judgement day.

The Reek towers majestically over the town of Westport where people say that if you can't see the summit, then it's raining and if you can see it, then it's going to rain. Such is the weather in the west of Ireland. Croagh Patrick had been a place of ritual and pilgrimage long before the advent of Christianity. It was once called Cruachán Aigli, the mountain of the eagle and there is a suggestion that the old Irish god Lugh resided upon the summit of the mountain and that he would change into the form of an eagle and fly over County Mayo. Pagans celebrated the harvest festival of Lughnasadh, which was held in honour of Lugh, and these celebrations were often held in high places. This tradition became absorbed into Christian beliefs and the festival is now celebrated by Christians on the last Sunday in July and called either Garland Sunday or Reek Sunday. The coat of arms of Westport incorporates an eagle.

In AD 1106 the Bishop of Ardpatrick was struck by lightning and killed whilst climbing the reek. Seven years later in 1113 a thunderbolt described as 'a ball of fire' was recorded as killing thirty pilgrims on the eve of St Patrick's festival as they fasted and prayed on the summit of the Reek. This terrible tragedy didn't stop people making the pilgrimage but as the years went on there was a shift away from climbing the Reek during Lent and on St Patrick's Day. The clergy simply decided to change the timing of the annual pilgrimage to the summer months of July and August when the weather was much more favourable.

St Patrick and Crom Dubh

Crom Dubh, or Crom Cruach as he is sometimes known, was depicted as a cruel tyrannical chieftain, a powerful magician, or a god. He is always represented as an opponent of Christianity and especially St Patrick. Crom Dubh means 'Black Crooked One'. He was an ancient god of fertility and the harvest in Ireland and had strong connections with Croagh Patrick in County Mayo.

The people of the area were so terrified of Crom and his two sons that if they heard the bark of his two hounds they fled in fear. Crom Dubh was said to be accompanied by a *leannán sidhe* (love fairy) who would advise him whether people were telling him the truth or not when it came to paying their rent to him. Anyone suspected of lying was brought before him the next day and he would pass judgement upon them. They were always found guilty and the punishment was always the same: death by fire.

The people tried many times to kill Crom but his *leannán sidhe* always knew their plans and protected Crom. The people began to believe that Crom Dubh was a demon that looked and walked like a man and they would have parted with all they owned if only someone could slay him and his sons and put an end to their evil ways but every attempt met with failure and the death of those involved. Each year was worse than the last and had no other option but to bend to his will. They even accepted the fact that it was Crom Dubh who was responsible for giving them what little they had: the light of the sun, the darkness of night and the changing seasons.

It was at this time that Patrick was travelling through Ireland, preaching the new religion and baptising people. He explained to those he met that his new God would be the light of the world and banish the darkness of evil. Some of those he spoke to began to listen. He was baptising some new followers one day at the Well of the Branch, now renamed Tobar Phádraig or Patrick's Well. They told him of Crom Dubh and begged him to ask the new God for help. Patrick was horrified when he heard of the terrible things that Crom Dubh was doing and set out immediately to confront him

St Patrick offered to convert Crom and his two sons to Christianity; however, Crom was a powerful druid and had no intention of renouncing his beliefs for this new religion. He was so angry at Patrick's offer that he set his hounds on him, which very nearly resulted in the death of the cleric. In order to protect himself, Patrick drew a circle on the ground with his staff. As soon as the hounds entered the circle, they became so gentle that they even licked Patrick's feet. Crom was incensed and caused a mighty fire to appear. He rushed at Patrick, intending to throw him into the flames, just as he had thrown others who had angered him into the flames. Patrick lifted a rock, made the sign of the cross over it and threw it into the middle of the fire. The moment it entered the flames, the fire sank down into the ground in such a way that the hole it left behind can still be seen to this day. The hole is called Poll na Seantainne. When Crom Dubh saw the fire had disappeared and the hounds had become docile in front of Patrick, he ran to his fort. Patrick followed and tried to talk to Crom Dubh because he still felt that it was possible to convert him to the new religion and to get him to renounce his evil ways, but Crom Dubh refused to listen and tried to use every trick he could to defeat Patrick, including magic, witchcraft and druidism, but none of these had any effect for Patrick's new God was far more powerful than Crom Dubh and his *leannán sidhe*.

Patrick then struck the ground with his staff, which caused the bridge to the sea stack to fall into the sea, leaving Crom and his sons marooned there for all time. It is said that they survived by eating seabirds and fish before eventually fading away, their power destroyed. The stack can still be found today, standing about one hundred and sixty feet high, located about three hundred feet off the Mayo cost near Ballycastle. Today it is called Downpatrick Head, but its Irish name is Dún Briste, which means 'broken fort'. All you will find on the stack now are hundreds of screeching gulls and the ancient ruins of an old fort.

To celebrate Patrick's victory over Crom Dubh, the locals hold a pattern day (a feast day) in honour of St Patrick at Downpatrick on the last Sunday of July, called in Irish *Domhnach Chruim Dubh*, 'Crom Dubh's Sunday'.

Downpatrick Head also featured in the 1798 rebellion, when twenty-five men lost their lives within Poll na Seantainne, a prominent blowhole. They are said to have hidden from the English redcoats on the ledge at the bottom; however, the tide came in before the ladder could be replaced, trapping them below and condemning them to a watery grave.

The Caorthannach

Long, long ago, when man first emerged from the primordial swamp and struggled to walk upright, the *Caorthannach* was watching. It has been suggested that she was born deep within the molten core of the earth and there she waited until mankind was ready to be preyed upon by her offspring, particularly those humans who were susceptible to evil. She is called the 'fire spitter' in early Irish folklore and the 'devil's mother' in the Christian tradition.

One of the most famous stories concerning the *Caorthannach* concerns her battle with St Patrick on County Mayo's holy mountain, Croagh Patrick. The story goes that St Patrick fought with the *Caorthannach* on the summit of the Reek when he banished the snakes and demons from Ireland. He raised his holy staff and called down a mighty whirlwind that carried all the serpents and demons out of Ireland and consigned them to the depths of the Atlantic Ocean, never to return.

All, that is, except the *Caorthannach*. Patrick is said to have defeated her and confined her to a lake south of the mountain which bears her name, Lough na Corra, but she escaped and headed for the safety of Lough Derg. Patrick saw her, grabbed a horse and gave chase. The chase was long and arduous. The *Caorthannach* knew that Patrick would tire, grow thirsty and need to quench his thirst so she spat fire and poison into every well she passed. Patrick, realising what she had done, prayed for guidance. As he prayed his horse stumbled and threw Patrick to the ground. Where he landed, a well sprang up and Patrick was able to drink the un-poisoned water. His thirst now satisfied, Patrick gave chase once again but this time he took a shortcut and arrived at Lough Derg before the demon.

When the *Caorthannach* arrived at Lough Derg, she believed she had beaten Patrick and was preparing to enter the waters and swim down to her cave at the bottom of the lough, which is said to be a portal to the underworld, when he jumped out from behind a large rock. Some say that as they fought in the waters of the lough she swallowed Patrick whole but he tore himself free from her stomach, spilling her blood into the waters of the lough. It is because of this that the lough was given its name Lough Derg, meaning 'dark lough'. They will tell you that she now lies on the bottom of the lough and that Patrick succeeded in killing the devil's mother once and for all as she has never been seen in Ireland from that day to this.

꧁꧂

As with all tales of St Patrick there is another version of the *Caorthannach*'s demise. It begins when Patrick reached Tullaghan in County Sligo. His horse stumbled and threw Patrick from the ground his horse. As he fell his hand hit a stone and a well sprang up where he landed. After quenching his thirst, he then hid in a hollow behind Hawke's Rock and waited for the devil's mother to arrive. As she approached, he sprang from his hiding place and with one word banished her to the depths of the Atlantic Ocean. The swell she created flowed into the well and it is now known as a healing well. It is said that it is filled by the ebb and flow of the tide, first containing freshwater, then containing saltwater. The mark of St Patrick's hand and the imprint of his horse's hoof can still be seen on the stones by the well, which is called Hawke's Well.

However, there are others who will tell you that legend and folklore suggest that the *Caorthannach* is neither dead nor banished.

She simply waits patiently for her time to come again. After all she has nothing but time and she is well used to waiting silently, ever ready to take advantage of any opportunity to cause chaos, famine, or war. Her children walk the earth in many different guises and her son still sits upon his throne, ready to command his legions of hell.

St Marcán's Lough, Clew Bay, County Mayo

There are many stories concerning Croagh Patrick in County Mayo and the festival of Lughnasadh. However, there is a site that seems to have been overshadowed by the majesty of the sacred mountain: St Marcán's Lough at Rosclave on one of the inlets that make up the eastern part of Clew Bay. There is a holy well on the site that is still visited by some pilgrims around the 4 August; however, there was a time not that long ago when thousands would turn up by car or on horseback and leave offerings to ensure the safety of their cattle. These offerings would range from rolls of butter to money and people would also leave 'spancels' on the ground around the well, which were ropes used to hobble the legs of cattle to stop them from wandering.

The well was believed to cure various diseases of cattle. There was an area of boggy ground near the well that people would drive their cattle over. If an afflicted animal crossed the ground without tripping it was said to be cured but if it tripped then its days on this earth were numbered. There was a story which stated that if your cattle were dying of disease then you should leave a spancel on a rock near Marcán's Well to ensure that no more would die. The well's powers would work even if you took water from it back to your home and treated the sick animals with it there.

There is no historical reference to any priest called Marcán; however, the name derives from the Irish word '*marcach*', a rider or horseman, which is significant as there is a tradition of swimming horses across the bay to an island in August. This tradition seems to have taken place throughout Ireland at Lughnasadh and there are records of it taking place across the country, from Cork to Donegal. In Bohola, County Mayo, there is a small lake called Loughkeeran where horses were bathed at Lughnasadh and there is also a tradition of throwing rolls of butter into the lough and hanging spancels on the branches of nearby trees.

The traditions at St Marcán's Lough may be related to St Brigid, who had connections with the nearby church at Kilbride and who, according to local folklore, cursed Marcán after an argument. One version of the story tells us that the argument concerned a disagreement about the milking of cows. One day Marcán came to say mass for Brigid and some of her nuns. Brigid asked him to wait until she had finished milking the cow. When she had finished the milking and sent up to her house she found that Marcán had said mass.

'Why did you not wait as I asked you?' she asked him.

To which Marcán replied, 'I'll say mass when I like.'

Brigid was so outraged by his response that she cursed him and his church. She told him that she would pray for his church to be covered with a lake. Marcán responded by saying that if it was, then the water should have a cure for people. Brigid told him that the waters may contain a cure but it would be for animals and not people. Given St Brigid's association with animals – in particular cattle and fertility – this is not that surprising. What is surprising is that two members of the church should have so disliked each other that their argument ended with them cursing one another.

There is also a children's burial ground, or *cillín*, within the vicinity of St Marcán's Lough.

St Patrick and his Garron

When St Patrick came to Ireland with the intention of igniting the fires of the new religion, he was met by numerous obstacles, from demons to serpents. However, he believed that his God would protect him.

When he arrived in County Mayo, he was accompanied by his servant Fintan, a pious and humble man who was extremely faithful. As they travelled through Mayo, the demons and serpents fled before Patrick in fear. He and Fintan approached the Reek (Croagh Patrick). Fintan had gone a little further up the trail than Patrick and when the serpents saw he was unprotected they turned back and killed him. When Patrick eventually reached the spot where Fintan lay, he saw that his faithful servant was dead and he fell on his knees in grief. He prayed to his God to bring Fintan back to life. No sooner had the words left his mouth than Fintan sat up as good as ever, with no memory of having died. Patrick gave thanks to God saying, 'In God's name we will set up a church here as a sign of the great power of God and we will call it Achaidh Cobhair'. The village is now called Aughagower.

Patrick bought a garron (a type of horse or pony) for carrying rocks to build the church. He blessed the horse for he knew that this particular horse had never refused any load it had been asked to carry. He then employed workmen, masons and carpenters and set them to work building his church. The men soon felt hungry and began to complain that there was no food to eat. There was famine on the land at the time and food could not be found, no matter how much gold or silver was offered, and yet Patrick needed to feed his workers.

Now it just so happened that there was a man called Black Cormac living nearby and it was said that he had a barn full of meal. The following day, Patrick climbed onto his garron and, taking a few men with him, he went to pay Black Cormac a visit. When he arrived at Black Cormac's house, he asked him how much it would cost for as many bags of meal as his horse could carry. Black Cormac looked at the little horse and with a sneer on his face gave Patrick a price. Patrick told him he thought it was a bargain and handed over the money. Patrick then sent his men into the barn and told them to bring out the biggest sack of meal they could find and place it on the garron's back. Black Cormac laughed and said it would break the creature's back.

'Never mind,' Patrick said, and he told his men to 'keep loading up the bags until I tell you to stop'. They loaded bag after bag onto the horse's back until the poor horse looked like he was carrying a load the size of a small house.

'Drive on now,' Patrick told the garron and the horse trotted off as though he was carrying bags of feathers rather than heavy meal. Black Cormac was not amused. In fact he was so angry he had turned bright red.

'Bad luck and my curse on the lot of you; you have me ruined. Get off my property,' he shouted.

Shortly after this, the workmen asked Patrick if he could get them some meat. Meal was all well and good but heavy work required something a bit more substantial. Some of the men mentioned that they had heard that Black Cormac had a bull that he was planning on selling for a cheap price so Patrick decided to send for him. He asked him how much he wanted for the bull. Now what no one knew was that the bull was extremely savage and had killed a number of Black Cormac's farmhands. Cormac now hated Patrick for getting the better of him and he hoped that the bull would kill him.

'You can have the bull for nothing but you must catch him yourself,' he told Patrick.

Patrick was delighted.

'I'm very grateful to you, Cormac,' he said, 'I'll come back for him this evening when we have finished work.'

That evening Patrick arrived at Black Cormac's house and asked him to show him the field in which the bull was kept. Cormac was delighted. He told Patrick to follow him as the field was nearby and they could walk together. He brought Patrick down a boreen and showed him the bull in the field.

Cormac turned to Patrick and with a cruel sneer on his face said, 'Go on take him now, if you dare.'

Patrick walked into the field. When the bull saw him, he raised his head and came charging towards him. Patrick raised his staff and made the sign of the cross between himself and the charging bull. The bull stopped, put his head down and followed Patrick out of the field like a gentle little lamb. Black Cormac nearly swallowed his teeth in anger.

When Patrick arrived back in Aughagower, he told his workmen to kill the bull and take the meat. However, they were to leave the skin and bones. A week later Black Cormac visited Patrick and asked to speak to him.

'I hear it said that you are an honest man, yet you have done me a great wrong,' said Cormac.

'How have I wronged you?' replied Patrick.

'You tricked me out of meal and a fine bull,' said Cormac.

'I gave you the full price agreed for the meal. As for the bull, you can have him back if he means that much to you," replied Patrick.

'How are you going to give me back my bull when your workmen have eaten it?' demanded Cormac.

Patrick called for his faithful servant Fintan and said to him, 'Bring me the skin and bones of the bull.'

Fintan returned with the skin and bones. Patrick prayed over them and in the blink of an eye the bull jumped up as fit and as well as the day he followed Patrick out of the field.

'Now Cormac, take your bull and be off with you.'

Black Cormac was astounded. He went straight home and told all who would listen that this man Patrick must be a great and powerful druid and that his bull must now be blessed. He explained that such a blessed bull must be worshipped as a god and the people agreed, saying they would return on Sunday morning. When Patrick heard what Black Cormac was telling people, he was very angry and threatened him, telling him not to spread such lies as they would lead the people astray from the true faith that Patrick was teaching them. Black Cormac refused to listen. On Sunday morning, some of the people turned up to worship the bull and Black Cormac decided to set an example by going into the field first. He prostrated himself on the ground in front of the bull, which promptly stuck both his horns into him and tossed him high into the air before trampling him to death. The people of Mayo still remember that day and call it Cormac Dubh's Sunday.

When Patrick had finished building his church in Aughagower, he said mass in it before heading to the Reek, where the serpents and demons had taken refuge. When he arrived at the bottom of the mountain, he dug a hole, then he climbed the Reek. He chased the serpents down to the hole, which by now had filled with water. They fell into the hole and all were drowned except for two that escaped. One of them went into a hole in a great rock near the Mouth of the Ford (Ballina) and caused great havoc with the people of that area.

Every night when the sun went down this serpent would light a candle and anyone who saw its light would fall down dead. The people called this serpent Sercín and the rock can still be seen to this day. It is called Carrig-Sercín. Patrick followed this serpent. He and Fintan arrived at a little village nearby and Patrick asked the widow woman who owned a lodging house for rooms for himself and Fintan.

'No problem but I'll have to lock the door before sunset,' she said.

'Why is that?' asked Patrick.

'There is a serpent that hides in a rock out at sea. He lights a candle every evening at sundown and whoever sees it dies. It is causing great heartbreak in the area.'

'Have you a candle in the house?' asked Patrick.

'Indeed I have not,' she replied.

'Have you the makings of a candle?' he asked.

'No, but I have some dry rushes if they are any use to you,' she said.

Patrick took out a sharp knife and cut a slice of fat from Fintan's stomach. He handed it to the widow woman and asked her to make a candle out of it. She did as he had asked and when the candle had been made, Patrick lit it and stood at the open door. It wasn't long before the serpent lit its own candle but no sooner was it lit than the serpent fell dead. The people were amazed and thankful. Patrick explained that it was through the power and love of his God that he had succeeded and he baptised each one of them.

The other serpent had escaped north to a little island. The name of this serpent was Bolán Mór or Big Bolaun and he was as big as a round tower. Patrick pursued him to a large lake but he had no boat with which to reach the island. He stripped down and, staff in hand, he swam out to the island. When the serpent saw him, he slithered into the water. As he approached Patrick, he opened his mouth and swallowed him whole. Patrick took out his knife and cut open the serpent's stomach. Bolán Mór began to bleed heavily, so heavily that the water of the lough turned red and from that day to this the lough is called Lough Dearg, meaning 'red lough'.

The following day, Patrick got into a boat with Fintan and a number of local villagers and they rowed out to the island. Patrick blessed it and the people decided to build a little monastery upon it and it has been a place of pilgrimage ever since.

Patrick stayed with the people for a time, but he missed Aughagower. When he arrived back, he was approached by a number of people who had heard the story about Black Cormac and the little garron. They offered him quite a deal of money for the little horse but Patrick refused to part with him.

One day the high king of Connacht came to Patrick and said, 'I hear you have a wonderful garron that is able to carry a heavy load.'

'He is a good garron. No load has ever failed him since I bought him and I wouldn't like to part with him,' replied Patrick.

'I'll give you as much gold as he is able to carry on his back in one day from sunrise to sunset. It's thirty miles from my castle to this place and he must do the journey in one day,' said the king.

'Perhaps you don't have as much gold in your house as my garron can carry,' replied Patrick.

'If I haven't, I'll give you as much gold as will fund the building of three churches and you will keep the garron,' offered the king.

'It's a bargain,' laughed Patrick.

'I'll remain here until morning and you can accompany me home,' he said to Patrick, 'you may stay there the night then return to Aughagower with your gold the following day.'

'Very well. Agreed,' said Patrick.

The next day they all headed off, the king and his servants riding in the royal coach and Patrick on his garron. The king ordered his horses to be driven as fast as possible to see if the little garron could keep up, but even if they had run ten times faster, the garron would have trotted alongside them, not even breathing heavily.

Patrick spent a comfortable night at the king's fort. He had a lovely sleep and a great Irish breakfast before he headed down to the royal treasury with his garron. The treasurer was already there with his men. They filled a great big sack with gold and placed it onto the garron's back

'Will he be able to carry that all the way back to Aughagower?' asked the king.

'Not a bother,' said Patrick, 'stick another on him.'

They filled bag after bag and loaded the poor horse till his legs would surely buckled.

'Surely he can take no more,' said the king.

'Arra, you haven't even started yet. Stick another one on him,' said Patrick.

Well, they loaded every bit of gold they could find in the treasury onto the garron, but Patrick still wasn't satisfied.

'Stick a few bags of iron on top of that,' he said.

They did as he ordered and then Patrick led the garron out of the treasury saying, 'Now didn't I tell you my little garron could carry as much as you had in your treasury and it still wouldn't amount to half a load?'

The king was astonished. He agreed with Patrick and told him he would honour their agreement. Patrick was given all the gold necessary to build three churches and he kept his garron. He returned to Aughagower and the garron carried every stone that went into the building of the churches. You may have heard the old saying 'May you have the strength of Patrick's garron'. When the churches were finished, Patrick gave his garron to the people of Aughagower before setting off on foot around Ireland, lighting the fire of the new faith.

19

GULEESH OF COUNTY MAYO

Once upon a time, long, long ago, there lived in County Mayo a young boy whose name was Guleesh. Unfortunately he was bone idle and spent his time daydreaming, expecting all the finer things in life to come knocking on his door rather than working for them – how many times have we heard of such people?

Not far from the gable end of his family cottage, there was a rath or ring fort and Guleesh spent many hours sitting on the earthen wall that surrounded it, whiling away the day smoking his little pipe and thinking of nothing in particular. One fine night he stood half leaning against the gable of the cottage, looking up at the stars and the moon.

'I'm fed up and sick and tired of this place,' he said to himself, 'nothing ever happens. If only I could get away from here, I'd never come back. Oh, if only I was like the moon travelling across the sky, I could please myself and I wouldn't have to answer to anyone.'

'I wish I was you,' Guleesh shouted up at the big silvery moon.

Well, the words had hardly left his mouth when he heard a great noise coming towards him. It sounded like many people running together, talking and laughing, voices raised in excitement. The sound rushed past him like a huge gust of wind. As Guleesh listened to the sound it seemed to move in the direction of the rath.

'Musha, that sounded like the *gaoithe sidhe*,' Guleesh whispered to no one in particular.

He decided to follow the sound.

The *gaoithe sidhe* was the fairy wind and although Guleesh had heard the old stories concerning the fairy folk, he didn't really understand the power of the fairy chant. He followed the sound into the rath and it was then he heard the voices of the gentry, as they were known, crying out, 'My horse, and bridle, and saddle! My horse, and bridle, and saddle!'

Guleesh was suddenly caught up in the excitement and before he knew what was happening he joined in the chant.

'My horse, and bridle, and saddle! My horse, and bridle, and saddle! My horse, and bridle, and saddle! My horse, and bridle, and saddle!'

Suddenly a beautiful black stallion appeared with gold and silver on its saddle. Guleesh jumped up onto its back and as soon as he was in the saddle he saw that the rath was full of horses with the gentry sitting upon them. One of the fairy folk approached Guleesh riding a horse the likes of which you've never seen. Both he and the horse were adorned in silver, gold and the finest of jewels. Guleesh knew without being told that this was the fairy king.

'Will you come with us?' the fairy king asked as he rode away.

'I will surely,' answered Guleesh as he followed with a wild look in his eyes.

On they rode with the wind carrying them on faster and faster, moving with the speed of a hundred hurricanes. They raced the cold winter wind and overtook her. The green fields of Ireland gave way to the sea. They rode the clouds, looking down upon the heaving waves and soon they were once again riding over dry land. The king spoke a magic spell and the fairy horde landed in the courtyard of a great castle. Guleesh looked around in confusion; he had no idea where he was when suddenly the fairy king spoke to him.

'We have entered the green fields of France; it is here in this castle that our business lies. Here dwells the most beautiful princess the sun ever laid eyes on. She is to be wed to a cruel and heartless nobleman and I intend to spirit her away with us to safety. However, she cannot ride with us as we are of the magical race. This is why I asked you to ride with us for you are flesh and blood and so she may ride behind you on your horse. It is against our laws for her to lay her hands upon us but she may grip tightly to you as we ride the wind. Will you do this for me, Guleesh?'

'I will, your honour,' replied Guleesh.

They got off their horses and one of the gentry uttered words that Guleesh could not understand. Suddenly they were all inside the palace. There was a great celebration going on, with feasting, music and dancing. No expense had been spared and Guleesh stood open-mouthed as he saw all the riches of the kingdom displayed before him. It appeared as if every nobleman and lady in France and beyond were there, dressed in the finest silks and jewels, satin, gold and silver.

However, all of this faded into nothing as the princess appeared. Her beauty took his breath away and he felt his heart miss a beat. She was the only child of the king of France and she was to be married to the son of another king that very night. The feast had already been going on for three days. The wedding was to take place on the third night, the very night that Guleesh and the fairy horde came, hoping to carry her off.

Guleesh and his companions were standing together at the end of the hall, where there was a marble altar with two bishops standing ready to carry out the wedding ceremony as soon as the time arrived. However, no one could see Guleesh or his companions because they had cast a spell as they entered the palace that made them all invisible.

Guleesh noticed that there was a tear rolling down the cheek of the princess. He turned to one of his companions and whispered, 'Why is she crying?'

'It is because her heart is breaking,' replied his companion. 'She is marrying a man she does not love. Her father was going to give her to this cruel and heartless man when she was only fifteen but she said she was too young and begged him for more time. He gave her a year but made her promise that when the year was up she would carry out his wishes. However, we have other plans for her and she will not marry some king's son tonight.'

Guleesh saw a look in the eye of his fairy companion that he did not like and began to have second thoughts about helping the fairy horde. He suspected that the princess would be no better off with either one or the other. He cursed the night he had promised to help snatch her away from her home and her father. He began thinking about what could he do to save her, but he could think of nothing.

When the music stopped and the dancing was over, the old king, her father, and her mother, the queen, came up and said that this was the time to carry out the wedding ceremony. The bishop stood ready. It was time to put the ring on her finger and give her to her new husband. The king took the groom by the hand and the queen took her daughter and they went towards the altar, followed by all the lords, ladies and gentlemen.

As they approached the altar, one of the fairy folk stretched out his leg and tripped up the princess. He quickly cast a spell and threw a magic cloak over her. She instantly disappeared before the startled eyes of all the guests. The fairies seized her and they flew out of the palace into the darkness of the night with the princess and Guleesh. With a cry of 'My horse, my bridle, and saddle', they began to vault onto their horses and race off towards Ireland. The fairy king called out to Guleesh, 'Jump up onto your horse and put the lady behind you and we will be on our way for the morning sun will soon rise.'

Guleesh placed the princess on his horse and told her to hold on tight.

'Rise, horse,' he cried and his horse rose into the air. They followed the fairy horde across the sea and back to the green land of Erin. On they rode until at last they came to the fairy rath and the home of Guleesh. It was here that Guleesh jumped from his horse and pulled the princess down with him.

'I call and cross you to myself, in the name of God!' he said.

No sooner were the words out of his mouth than the fine stallion he rode turned into a plough horse and the fairies' power faded.

'Guleesh, you thief, you traitor,' the fairies all called out together, 'may you never have any luck. Why have you played such an evil trick on us? You will never get away with this.'

The fairies could do nothing to get her back for Guleesh had called on the power of the new religion.

'Oh Guleesh,' the fairy king called out, 'isn't it a nice way to treat your friends after we were so kind to you? But heed my words, you will never be happy with your prize. You will rue the day you tricked the fairy horde of the rath.'

He then approached the princess and struck her a blow on the side of the head.

'Now, you fool, she will never speak another word for as long as she lives. What good will she be to you now that she's dumb? It's time for us to return to our rath, but you'll remember this night's work, Guleesh, you have my word for that.'

As he finished talking, he stretched out his hands and before Guleesh could answer him the fairy king and his companions were gone into the rath. He never saw them again.

'Thanks be to God they're gone,' Guleesh said to the princess, 'we're better off without them. Aren't you better off with me anyway? Now, come on home with me to my father's cottage. You may spend the night there and if there is anything I can do to make you comfortable, you need only ask.'

The princess did not reply but Guleesh saw a silent tear roll down her cheek.

'Lady,' Guleesh said, 'please tell me what to do. I was never one of those fairy people. I'm just the simple son of an honest farmer. I went with them without thinking. If I can get word to your father, I will and I pray that I'll be able to return you safely to him.'

She moved her mouth as if to speak but no words came out.

'It cannot be that you are dumb,' said Guleesh. 'Did that devil really rob you of speech when he struck the side of your head?'

She raised her hand to her mouth and laid a finger on her tongue to show him that she had lost her voice and power of speech. The tears started flowing once again. Guleesh felt his heart ache and he felt his own tears flow. He wondered how on earth he could ever explain things to his father and mother for he knew that they would not believe that he had been in France and brought the king of France's daughter back with him. He was afraid they might make fun of the young lady or insult her. It was then he remembered the village priest.

'Praise be to God,' said he, 'I know now what I'll do; I'll take her to the priest's house. He won't refuse to keep the lady and care for her.'

He turned to the lady again and told her that he was a little worried about taking her to his father's house, but that there was an excellent priest who had always been very friendly to him and who would take good care of her if she wished to remain in his house – and if there was anywhere else she would rather go, he said he would take her there.

She bent her head to show him that she agreed and that she was ready to follow him wherever he was going.

'We will go to the priest's house then,' said Guleesh. 'He owes me a few favours and will do anything I ask him.'

As they arrived at the house of the priest, the sun was just beginning to rise. Guleesh knocked hard on the door even though it was very early but as luck would have it the priest was an early riser and soon opened the door. When he saw Guleesh with the beautiful young girl, he smiled.

'Guleesh,' he said, 'couldn't you wait until the sun was a little higher in the sky to get married?'

'Father,' Guleesh answered, 'it's not marriage that I'm after. I came to ask you a favour. Will you please look after this young girl and give her lodging?'

'Come in and tell me all about it,' said the priest.

Once they were inside the house, Guleesh began to tell the priest his story and the priest was so surprised that he could not help calling out or clapping his hands together at times.

'I'm not telling a word of lie, nor making a joke of you,' said Guleesh, 'but it was from the palace of the king of France I carried off this lady and she is the daughter of the king of France.'

Guleesh said that he would be very thankful to the priest if he would keep her in his own house and the kind man said he would do that as long as Guleesh pleased, but that he did not know what they ought to do with her because they had no means of sending her back to her father again.

Guleesh answered that he was uneasy about the same thing but that he could think of nothing to do except to keep quiet until they could find an opportunity to do something better. They decided between themselves that the priest should tell anyone who asked that it was his brother's daughter who had come on a visit to him from another county and that he should tell everybody that she was dumb and do his best to keep everyone away from her. They told the young girl what it was they intended to do and she used her eyes to show that she agreed with them.

Guleesh went home then and when his family asked him where he had been, he said that he had been asleep at the foot of the ditch and had passed the night there.

There was great wonderment on the part of the priest's neighbours about the girl who came so suddenly to his house without anyone knowing where she was from or what business she had there. Some people said that everything was not as it ought to be while others said that Guleesh was not the same man that he had been before. Everyone agreed that it was a great story; how Guleesh was going every day to the priest's house and how the priest had a great respect for him, all of which was very unusual.

For almost a year, the princess lived with the priest, who believed the whole of Guleesh's incredible tale. Guleesh spent long hours trying to coax words from the silent girl. He recited stories and sang songs, he told her of his travels, he spoke as many words as he knew were in the world but the best he received from her was a smile and a nod. Rumours began to spread around the village that the priest had a secret wife. Of course, the truth was too strange to even be guessed at.

So the time passed and soon the anniversary of the night ride with the fairy horde came around. Guleesh was lying by himself on the grass near his home. It was the last day of autumn and he was thinking of all that had happened in the year since he had crossed the sea.

'What if I stand in the same spot as before,' he suddenly thought to himself, 'maybe the fairy horde will ride again and I might see or hear something useful that might bring back Mary's voice.'

Mary was the name that he and the priest had given the princess.

He ran to the house of the priest and told him of his plan. The priest gave him his blessing and warned him to be careful.

Guleesh went to the old rath as the night grew darker and he stood with his bent elbow leaning on a grey old flag, waiting till the middle of the night came. The moon rose slowly and it shone like a ball of fire behind him. There was a white fog that seemed to cover the fields like a silver blanket. The night was as calm as a lake when there is not a breath of wind to move a wave on it and there was no sound to be heard but the drone of the insects that would go by from time to time or the hoarse screams of the wild geese. There were a thousand bright stars shining over his head and there was a little frost, which left the grass underfoot white and crisp.

He stood there for an hour, then two, then three, and it got colder and colder. He was beginning to think that maybe this wasn't the best idea he had ever had and that the fairies wouldn't leave their rath this night when he heard a far away sound coming towards him, and he recognised it immediately. The sound grew louder. At first it was like the beating of waves on a stony shore, then like the falling of a great waterfall, and at last it was like a loud storm in the tops of the trees before a whirlwind containing the fairy horde burst forth from the rath.

The whirlwind went past him at such speed that it took his breath away. He listened, hoping to hear the voices as before, when suddenly he heard the fairy folk cry out.

'My horse, and bridle, and saddle! My horse, and bridle, and saddle!'

Guleesh called out as loudly as any of them, 'My horse, and bridle, and saddle! My horse, and bridle, and saddle!'

However, just as the words left his mouth another voice cried out, 'Guleesh, my boy, are you here with us again? How are you getting on with your woman? There's no use in your calling for your horse tonight for I'll tell you this: you won't play such a trick on us again. It was a good trick you played on us last year.'

'It was,' said another man, 'he won't do it again.'

'Isn't he a prime lad, the same lad?' said the third man. 'To take a woman with him who never said as much to him as "How do you do?" since this time last year!'

'Perhaps he likes to be looking at her,' said another voice.

'That's true for you.'

'He is an *amadán*.'

'Don't bother your head with him; come on, let's get going.'

'We'll leave the eejit as he is.'

'If the *amadán* only knew that there's a herb growing up by his own door and if he were to boil it and give it to her, she'd be well,' said another voice and Guleesh recognised it as the voice of the fairy king. 'Brew up a broth, bid your lady to drink it and let this be the last time we ever see you.'

With that they rose up into the air and in the blink of an eye they were gone. They left Guleesh standing where they found him, looking after them and wondering. He didn't stand there for long. He began to think about all he had heard and started to wonder if there really was a herb growing by his own door that would bring back the power of speech to the princess.

'It can't be,' Guleesh said to himself. 'Why would they tell me if there was any truth in it? Unless he wasn't thinking ... Perhaps the fairy king didn't intend to let the word slip out of his mouth. I'll search the ground as soon as the sun rises. I'll see whether there's any plant growing beside the house except thistles and dock.'

He went home and even though he was tired he couldn't sleep a wink. As soon as the sun rose the following morning, Guleesh was out searching for any herb he didn't recognise. To his surprise, he found one growing next to the gable of the cottage.

He went over to it and looked at it closely. He saw that there were seven little branches coming out of the stalk with seven leaves growing on every small branch and a white sap in the leaves.

'It's very curious that I never noticed this herb before,' said Guleesh.

He drew out his knife, cut the plant and carried it into his own house. He stripped the leaves from it and cut up the stalk. A thick, white juice came out of it. He put it in a little pot with some water and placed the pot on the fire. When the water began to boil, he took a cup, filled half of it with the juice and put it to his own mouth. It came into his head then that perhaps it was poisonous and that the good people were seeking revenge, only tempting him so he might kill himself with it or put the girl to death without meaning it.

He put the cup down again, raised a couple of drops on the top of his finger and put it to his mouth. It was not bitter and indeed had a sweet, agreeable taste. He grew bolder then and drank a full thimble of it and then as much again. He didn't stop till he had half the cup drunk. He fell asleep after that and did not wake till it was night. When he awoke, there was great hunger and great thirst on him.

He had to wait, then, till daybreak, but he determined that as soon as he should wake in the morning he would go to the princess and give her a drink of the herb juice. As soon as he got up in the morning, he went over to the priest's house with the drink in his hand. He felt marvellous. In fact, he had never felt better and he was quite certain that it was the drink which made him feel so fantastic.

When he came to the house, he found the priest and the young lady within. They were wondering why he had not visited them for two days.

He told them all his news. He told them that he was certain that there was great power in that herb and that it would not harm the princess as he had tested it upon himself with no ill effects; in fact, he had never felt better. He then asked the princess to taste it. He gave his word that there was no harm in it. Guleesh handed her the cup and she drank half of it. She then fell back on her bed in a deep sleep. She slept until late the following day.

She awoke at last, rubbed her eyes and sat up. The two men were extremely nervous as they waited to see whether or not she would speak. She looked like a person who didn't know where she was. When they had been silent for a couple of minutes, the priest spoke to her.

'Did you sleep well, Mary?'

'I slept,' she answered him, 'thank you.'

No sooner had Guleesh heard her talking than he jumped up with a great shout of joy, ran over to her and fell on his two knees.

'A thousand thanks to God, who has given you back your voice,' he said, 'lady of my heart, speak again to me.'

The princess thanked him from the bottom of her heart for all the kindness he had shown her since the day she first came to Ireland and that she never would forget it.

Guleesh was absolutely delighted. They brought her food and she ate as if she hadn't eaten for a week, laughing and talking with the priest while she was eating. Guleesh went home to his house, stretched himself out on the bed and fell asleep again. The herb he had taken had not yet fully worn off and he slept for a full day and a night. When he woke up, he went back to the priest's house and found that the young lady was in the same state. She had been asleep almost since the time that he left the house.

He went into her room with the priest and they remained watching her until she awoke the second time. She had her voice back as strong as ever. Guleesh was very happy and the priest put food on the table again and they ate together. Guleesh came to visit her every day and the friendship that was between him and the princess blossomed. Eventually they realised that they loved each other and their marriage took place. The ceremony was performed by their friend, the priest, of course and as far as I know they lived happily ever after, for isn't that the way a story should end?

20

CILLÍNÍ

A *cillín* is an unconsecrated place used for the burial of babies. Being unbaptised, they were considered unsuitable by the Roman Catholic Church for burial in consecrated ground. Instead they were buried between sunset and sunrise outside the walls of a graveyard or even in graveyards that were no longer used.

This custom seems to have been common practice throughout Ireland until the nineteenth century, particularly in the west of the country. *Cillíní* were usually located at sites that had a sacred or religious association but children were also buried at crossroads, ring forts and even at the seashore. It was said that a little coffin would be brought at night by the father or grandfather and the only sign that a burial had taken place was a newly made grave. Mothers were not allowed to hold their babies or to be present at the burial and it wasn't unknown for mothers to live and die never knowing where their child had been buried.

The souls of the little babies were said to be cursed to carry a candle forever. These baby-lights were often seen at night outside graveyards, especially in the month of November. People were led to believe by the religious that the lonely little souls were searching for their parents or relations inside the graveyards but they could never enter as they were unbaptised.

As recently as fifty years ago in some areas, unbaptised babies were buried in the path around a graveyard. Parents did not go to the grave with the dead child, particularly if it was their first child. They believed that if they brought one child to the grave they would bring the next and possibly all their children there also. Should more than two infants from the same family be born dead, the cycle could be broken by changing the place in which the infants were buried.

However, folklore tells us that it wasn't just children that were buried in *cillíní*. Adults, particularly strangers whose religion was unknown or suicides, were sometimes buried in these areas. The list of those considered undesirable included executed criminals, unmarried mothers who died in childbirth, the mentally ill and even shipwrecked sailors. The Ordnance Survey recorded the continued use of children's burial grounds and an example of the custom was recorded in County Mayo as recently as 1964.

Although considered to be a throwback to a time when the Catholic Church was extremely repressive, *cillíní* date back to a time when our pagan customs were entwined with Christianity. Today many towns and villages are reclaiming these long-forgotten burial places back into the community. We will never know how many adults and children were buried within *cillíní*. We will never know the grief and shame of those poor unfortunates who were forced by those who should have known better, etched upon their souls for the rest of their lives. Hopefully one day we may see a memorial in every town and village so that we can pay our respects to those who lie in those lonely and, for the most part, forgotten places.

21

IRISH
WAKES

Wakes of times gone by began with women washing the body of the deceased and preparing it to be laid out on a bed or a table, often in the largest room of the house. Clocks were stopped at the time of death. Mirrors were turned around or covered and curtains closed. The body was covered in white linen adorned with black or white ribbons or with flowers for the body of a child and lit candles were placed around the body.

Clay pipes, tobacco and snuff were also placed in the room. Every male caller was expected to take at least a puff as it was believed that the smoke kept evil spirits from finding the deceased. Usually a pipe and tobacco were place on a table next to the body. Occasionally a pipe was laid on the chest of the deceased male. Most of the clay pipes used in County Mayo were manufactured in Knockcroghery, County Roscommon. These pipes were called dudeens. They were short pipes, smoked by both men and women. After the wake was over, the pipe would be thrown away. Today, these clay pipes are frequently dug up in gardens. The use of snuff was also a custom at wakes in the region. A large tobacco and snuff factory was established in 1801 in Ballina, County Mayo, bringing great wealth and many jobs to the town.

Once the body was prepared, it was never left alone until after the burial. Someone, usually a woman, sat in the same room until it was taken away. According to custom, crying (keening) couldn't begin until after the body was prepared, just in case the sound might attract evil spirits that would take the soul of the departed. However, once the body was properly prepared, the keening began. Often family members would give the deceased a kiss goodbye.

In ancient times it was the duty of the bard, who was attached to the family of each chief or noble, assisted by some of the household, to raise the funeral song, but as times moved on this may have been entrusted to hired mourners, who were paid according to how well they performed. However, in much more recent times, it is the *caointhe*, the lead keener, who would be the first to lament the deceased. Keeners, especially the *caointhe*, recited poetry lamenting the loss of the loved one, in addition to crying and wailing. All the women in the house joined in, especially as each new caller arrived to pay his or her respects.

Wakes lasted two or three nights. Food, tobacco, snuff and liquor were plentiful. Out in the countryside, the liquor served consisted of whiskey or poteen (a very potent and illegal Irish homemade brew). Laughter and singing, as well as crying, filled the air as mourners shared humorous stories involving the deceased. In addition to this seeming merriment, games were played. While this may appear to have been disrespectful to the dead, it was not the intention. It is thought that the merrymaking aspects of these wake customs were influenced by our pagan heritage as well as the need to stay awake for such a long period of time. The Church frowned on these activities and tried hard to discourage the people from indulging in them. They even attempted to ban food and alcohol. Thankfully they were unsuccessful.

Between the extremes of tears and laughter, heartfelt poetical lamentations and boisterous songs, there were debates. As the mourners gathered round the kitchen table, poteen- or whiskey-laden tea in hand, it was inevitable that discussions would begin. Often these debates turned heated, as one might expect given that the most common topics concerned religion, politics or economics.

An Irish wake is a traditional way of celebrating the deceased person's life. There have been changes over the years. Most wakes are now not as formal as they used to be and most have given up the tradition of having the body displayed in their home. People may now choose to hold the wake in the pub or another public area, such as a local hotel, without the deceased present. You may still hear of a house wake, although they are getting rarer.

In some parts of Ireland traditions are still very important. I have been to a number of wakes in my life and I have seen how important it is for the family of the deceased to make sure that their loved one gets a good send-off. I believe it is extremely important for us to stand by our traditions as they bind us together and help us at certain times to cope with the stresses of a modern society.

Superstition Surrounding Death

When someone dies, you should close the curtains in the room in which the death took place and the body lies. This is done to prevent a moonbeam shining through the window onto the corpse or coffin, allowing the devil to send his demons down along the moonbeam to steal the soul.

All clocks are stopped at the time of death to confuse the devil and give the soul time to reach heaven.

In Ireland the dead are carried out of the house feet first in order to prevent the spirit from looking back into the house and beckoning another member of the family to follow.

Family photographs are also turned face down or against the wall to prevent any of the close relatives and friends of the deceased from being possessed by the dead.

All the mirrors in the house are covered at the time of death to prevent the soul from being trapped in a mirror.

Never wear something new to the funeral, especially shoes.

It was also said to be bad luck for a pregnant woman to attend a funeral in case her baby would be born dead or deformed. It was believed that a condition known as club foot was caused by the mother slipping or stumbling in the graveyard. There is a story told about one lady who was foolish enough to go to a funeral when she was heavily pregnant. She leaned against a headstone and when her baby was born it had a birthmark in the shape of a headstone on its back. The teller of this story swore it to be true 'by the help of God'. Pregnant women were even told not to remain in a house while a corpse was being placed in the coffin nor act as a sponsor to a bride.

The souls of those who happen to die abroad greatly desire to rest in Ireland. Their relations consider it their duty to bring back the body to be laid in Irish earth. However, even then the dead may not rest peaceably unless laid with their ancestors and not amongst strangers.

A young girl happened to die of a fever while away on a visit to some friends and her father thought it safer not to bring her home but to have her buried in the nearest cemetery because in those days fever was greatly feared. A few nights after returning home he was woken up by a mournful wailing at his bedroom window. He heard a voice crying out, 'I'm alone, I'm alone, so alone'. The poor man knew well what it was and he prayed in the name of God that the spirit of his dead child might rest in peace until the morning. At daybreak the following morning he rose from his bed and set off to the strange burial place of his daughter and there he drew the coffin from the ground. He had it placed upon a cart and transported back to County Mayo. After he had the coffin re-buried beside her own people, the spirit of his child appeared to be at rest for her mournful cry was never heard again.

Finally the custom of placing candles on or around the coffin at a wake comes from the belief that you were lighting the way to paradise for the deceased. This continued as you walked with the coffin to its final resting place. The tradition of walking slowly behind or on either side of the coffin came about because you walked slowly so the candles would not blow out. You see, there is always a simple explanation.

The ends of candles used at a wake were said to be able to cure burns.

22

THE
YEW

COUNTY MAYO (MAIGH EO),
'PLAIN OF THE YEW TREES'

The coat of arms of County Mayo bears nine yew trees. 'Mayo' is anglicised from the Irish '*Maigh Eo*', meaning 'the plain of the yew trees' and the nine yew trees express that fact with one for each barony of the county.

Trees have always had a special place in myth and religion and the Irish language even has a special word for the sacred tree, '*bile*' (pronounced 'bee-lay'). Academics, artists, ecologists and dreamers all look at a tree and each see something different, yet none can create it; only time and nature is capable of that miracle. The tree has the power to inspire. It gives us shelter and in some cases it provides us with food. Like stone, it stands as a silent witness to the passing of years, witnessing all that transpires. It is a thing of great beauty, romance and mystery and, for those who believe in superstition, it can summon the revenge of the fairies and the anger of the gods.

In Ireland we used to be well aware of the majesty of the tree and the respect it commanded. Trees were granted protection under Brehon Law. Unfortunately modern Ireland has become far more primitive in its understanding of the natural world and its environment as we achieve ever more financial success. Irish spirituality has suffered as a result and although a violent storm may fell a tree, only man will cut down a whole forest in the name of profit and progress. Pre-Christian Ireland had its share of sacred trees. A specific tree not only served as a landmark; it often made a place special. One such tree is the yew.

There is quite a bit of evidence in folklore and mythology indicating that yews were venerated. They are our largest native evergreen and when they grow in mixed woodland, the shade they cast and the toxins they secrete in their root systems create an open clearing – the ideal place for a ceremony. Our ancestors also seem to have been impressed by the fact that they remained green and vibrant when all the other large trees had succumbed to winter. The yew is the longest-living tree and was once thought to be immortal. They therefore became associated with victory over death.

It is also known as a guardian, forming the gateway pillars to the other world. It protects the dead and is linked to kingship and war due to its use in making bows and spears. It could also be used to make wands.

When a pagan burial was carried out in times gone, a sprig of yew was placed on the deceased person's chest and it has been suggested that by this could have resulted in some of those sprigs propagating in the same way a gardener would propagate a cutting nowadays. These would eventually grow in these burial areas, thus marking them out as burial sites. There may or may not be some truth in this. It is an interesting idea though.

Staves of yew were kept in Irish pagan graveyards where they were used for measuring corpses and graves. The wood or leaves were laid on graves as a reminder to the departed spirit that death was only a pause in life before rebirth. The yew's long life is due to the unique way in which the tree grows. Its branches grow down into the ground to form new stems, which then rise up around the old central growth as separate but linked trunks. After a time, they cannot be distinguished from the original tree. It is for this reason that the yew has always been a symbol of death and rebirth, the new that springs out of the old.

When the Christians built on sacred pagan sites, these trees would already be present, which accounts for very old yews in places where churches were erected hundreds of years ago. Choosing to build an abbey round a yew tree is one of many examples of the Christianisation of much older pagan beliefs.

Most pagans view death as a passage rather than an ending, something to be celebrated and not feared or despised. Death is such a fundamental process in nature that, without it, life could

not exist. Life constantly changes into death and each moment of death is a moment of rebirth. There are beginnings and endings, but the flow of existence is never-ending.

Unfortunately this view is not shared by the mainstream Christian religions so the cemetery is nowadays looked upon as a place of fear rather than a sacred place of return to the ancestral realm.

The yew itself has particular qualities which evoke a feeling of awe in those who find themselves in its presence. The natural yew forests that still cover parts of Europe are places with an intense feeling in the atmosphere. In the early morning mists, such vast forests become forbidding places that can give a strange sense of unease to a modern-day visitor, let alone a hapless pagan, who would have been at the mercy of natural forces as well as being of simpler mind and understanding. We have hard evidence, from bog wood and studies of fossil pollen, that yews were once much more widespread in Ireland than they are today and the probable reason for their decline is that they were destroyed by humans. Yew foliage is quite poisonous to livestock (and humans) and, while we may have revered yew trees, over the millennia we have shown that we revere cattle and horses even more.

An old folk tale tells why yews are dressed so darkly:

When the yew was a young species, in times when there were few people, it was thought that all other trees were more beautiful, for their colourful leaves could flutter in the wind unlike the stiff pine needles of the yew tree. Thinking that the faeries had deliberately made it unattractive, the tree pined. However, the faeries wanted to please the yew and it woke one sunny morning to find its needles had changed to leaves of gold and its heart jumped with joy. Some thieves came and stole the leaves, making the tree confused and sad, so the fairies tried again and gave it leaves of pure crystal and the yew loved its sparkle, but a storm of hail came and the crystals shattered. Then they gave it broad leaves and it waved them in the air only to have them eaten by goats. At this, the yew gave up for it realised that its original dress was by far the best, for it was one of permanence, long ages and deep knowledge, and in this the tree found comfort.

23

WHO WAS THE
HANGMAN OF
ROBERT EMMET?

In 1878 an old man lay dying in the Ballina workhouse in County
Mayo. His name was Barney Moran and it is thought that he was
born in 1779, which would have put him at 98 or 99 years old.
He had a hard life. Born in the ruins of an old dwelling near Castlebar
to a travelling woman, he joined the British Army at the age of 16.
Perhaps he thought that at least there he would get fed and sheltered
instead of having to beg for a living so who are we to judge? If he was
in fact born in or around 1779, then at the age of 16 it would have
been about 1795, so he may have witnessed the 1798 Rebellion and
the French marching on Castlebar. He would have seen all the different colours of the French uniforms and flags and the well-trained
soldiers as they marched to the sound of the drummer boys. He may
even have been among the British redcoats as they fled the town of
Castlebar in what became known as the 'Races of Castlebar'.

He was later to claim that while in a Dublin prison, awaiting death for the murder of a comrade, he was approached by a

British government agent who offered him a pardon if he agreed to carry out an execution. He agreed to the request, although he denied that he knew the identity of the person to be executed; all he would say was that he looked like a leader of men. It was on 20 September 1803 in Thomas Street, Dublin, that Robert Emmet was hanged in public. Moran claimed that he would not have been recognised by any of those gathered as he had a heavy beard and was wearing a hangman's hood.

When he returned to County Mayo years later, he took up residence near St Patrick's church. Some of the locals still refer to the road where he lived as 'Barney's road'. He was looked upon as a bit of an eccentric, a harmless old man who was given the odd bit of charity and kindness by those who lived locally. He was known to be a bit of a singer of ballads and he played a tin whistle, performing at street markets and the odd fair. Some of the ballads he sang were about the great Irish patriot, Robert Emmet.

Eventually Barney Moran felt his life was slipping away. He had no family so, like many others before and since, he ended up in the workhouse in Ballina. It is said that on his deathbed he asked for two local businessmen he trusted to take his confession; however, he swore them to secrecy, asking that they say nothing until after his death. He told them of the part he played in Emmet's execution; he said that Emmet did not blame him personally as he was only doing his job. His death wish was honoured. It wasn't until after his funeral that news of his involvement in Emmet's death spread around the town and many of the locals were outraged and revolted that this man to whom they had shown kindness and charity had such a hand in the killing of an Irish hero. Some of them went as far as digging up his coffin and driving spikes into it. Despised by his own countrymen and disowned by the British government he served so well, his only reward was a lonely death in a workhouse and an unmarked pauper's grave in Leigue cemetery near Ballina. Ironically, some of his neighbours include the hunger strikers, Frank Stagg and Michael Gaughan, who gave their lives in pursuit of Irish freedom.

Could this be a true story or is it just the ramblings of a poor old man who wanted to be remembered for something, to leave a legacy behind? History tells us that Emmet's executioner was Thomas Galvin. However, because his alleged crime was that of high treason against the Crown, Emmet was to be beheaded and it is this extra act that may explain why Barney Moran claimed to have been involved. An eyewitness account of the day tells of the final act. Thomas Galvin had been provided with an axe and a sharp knife with which to perform his gruesome duty. He cut down the body of Robert Emmet, laid it upon the scaffolding planks and proceeded to cut around Emmet's neck. He cut one side but was having difficulty turning the body over to access the other side so asked the sheriff who was in attendance to procure him some assistance from the crowd of onlookers. A man dressed in the clothes of a countryman was forced up on stage at bayonet point and made to give Galvin the help he needed. Could this countryman have been Barney Moran? Did he exaggerate the part he played as he wished to make himself seem more important in death than he had been in life? I suppose we will never know, so the mystery remains and will never be solved.

There is another interesting twist to the final story of Robert Emmet and it concerns the man who presided over the trial. He was one of the most hated and reviled men in Ireland at that time and his name was John Toler.

LORD NORBURY, THE HANGING JUDGE

John Toler was born in County Tipperary in 1745. He was admitted to the bar in 1770 and, as a strong supporter of the government, he attained many offices, including that of Lord Chief Justice, and was eventually ennobled as the Earl of Norbury. He was also the Solicitor General and a member of Grattan's Parliament. Later, by bribery and deception, he reached the bench and became a corrupt and fearsome judge. He had poor legal skills and used his power, his sarcastic wit and his twisted sense of humour to intimidate lawyers and defendants. His courts were like a wild theatre. His most famous trial was that of Robert Emmet (1803), in which

Norbury continually interrupted and abused Emmet when he was making his speech from the dock before sentencing him to death.

Daniel O'Connell despised him and initiated the investigation into his conduct during a trial in which he fell asleep. He was eventually removed from the bench in 1827 due to his absent-mindedness and his inclination to fall asleep during important trials. He died in his home, No. 3 Great Denmark Street, Dublin, on 27 July 1831 at the age of 85 years and was buried at St Mary's church, Mary Street, Dublin.

However, there is an interesting twist to the story of Lord Norbury. It is said that Norbury wrongfully convicted an innocent young man from Blanchardstown of the capital crime of sheep-stealing. The man was hanged and his distraught widow survived him by just a few months. On her deathbed she cursed Norbury, vowing to haunt him until the end of time, promising that she would never let him have another night's sleep. Norbury was said to have suffered from chronic insomnia after that, a deserving end to a brutal man. Upon his own death, Norbury was reportedly changed into a phantom black hound, condemned to forever roam the streets of Cabra, dragging a hefty chain in his wake. Is this a shaggy dog story or has it some basis in truth? I suppose we'll never know.

FESTIVALS

IMBOLC, THE FESTIVAL OF BRIGID

In the ancient, agrarian society of the Celts, the heralding of spring was no small thing as people would have spent months in the frigid cold, often with little food stores left. Imbolc is a word believed to be derived from the Old Irish '*Imbolg*' which translates as 'in the belly', referring to the pregnancy of ewes, an event which coincided with the onset of spring. Initially celebrated on 1 February, the festival of Brigid represented the point in the Celtic year that divided winter in half, when the crone aspect of the cold months receded, heralding the return of the young spring maiden. The festival of Imbolc celebrates the increasing strength of the new God, still in his child form, and a return of the maiden aspect of the goddess in the form of Brigid.

As the time of year that is full of energy, when the fertility of the land bursts forth, spring is full of the promise of renewal and potential, an awakening of the earth and its life force, and the return of the light and warmth of the sun and life's insatiable appetite for rebirth. It is time to let go of the past and to look to the future, a clearing out of the old, making both outer and inner space for new beginnings. This can be done in numerous ways, from spring cleaning your home to clearing the mind and heart to allow inspiration to enter and it is a good time to make a dedication to the goddess Brigid. Imbolc is traditionally the great festival and honouring of Brigid (also known as Brighid, Bride or Brigit). She is a goddess of healing, poetry and smithcraft. She is a goddess of fire, the sun and the hearth and is associated with wells and water. She brings fertility to the land and its people and is closely connected to midwives and newborn babies. Fire and purification are an important aspect of this festival.

This is also the time to hang strips of cloth on the branches of a tree, rowan or willow if possible but if not then any tree near your house will serve the same purpose. The dew that settles on them overnight will be blessed by the goddess as she passes by and will

be imbued with the powers of healing and protection and these powers will last throughout the year. Keep them in a special place in the house and bring them out when needed. They could be wrapped around the site of pain or injury and in times gone by were used by midwives to help women in childbirth. These healing cloths can also be used on sick animals, especially cows and sheep.

Brigid's cross is made annually from straw or rushes and hung above the door. In pre-Christian times, it was probably a sun symbol and celebrated the power of the goddess to bring back the light at the Celtic feast of Imbolc. It holds the promise of fertility and abundance.

Symbols attributed to Brigid

The Snowdrop: The first gift of spring in the bleakness of winter.

The Swan: The swan mates for life and represents loyalty, fidelity and faithfulness. Swan feathers are a powerful amulet.

The Flame: Imbolc is a Fire Festival and fire of all kinds is associated with Brigid – the fire of creativity, the protective hearth fire and her fire wheel – Brigid's cross, which heralds her as a sun goddess.

Brigid's Cross: This is a traditional fire wheel symbol found at the hearths of homes throughout Ireland and beyond as a symbol of protection.

Brigid Doll: A very old tradition involved the making of a Brigid doll which can be included in ceremonies and/or placed in the 'bride's bed' to bring fertility and good fortune to the home.

The Serpent: In Celtic mythology, Brigid was associated with the awakening of a hibernating serpent which emerged from its lair at Imbolc. Traditionally serpents were associated with creativity and inspiration.

Sheep: Brigid's festival is at the beginning of lambing.

Herbs of Imbolc

Blackberry: Sacred to Brigid, the leaves and berries are used to attract prosperity and healing.

Coltsfoot: Coltsfoot or '*sponnc*' (Gaelic) is a herb associated with Brigid. A herb of Venus, it moves emotional and physical stagnation and is used magically to engender love and to bring peace.

Ginger: It revitalises and stimulates the 'fire within'.

Trees of Imbolc

Rowan: Luis, or the rowan, is the tree usually assigned to this time of year in the Celtic (ogham) tree alphabet. It has long been associated with the maiden aspect of the triple goddess. It is also known as the 'quickening tree' and is associated with serpents. Traditionally it protects and wards off evil. A sprig of rowan can be put near the door of your home or worn for protection. Rowan berries have a tiny five-pointed star on the bottom, reminiscent of the pentagram.

Willow: The fourth tree in the Celtic tree alphabet is also long-associated with the maiden aspect of the triple goddess. Willow is the great 'shape-shifter' of consciousness and emotion and symbolises feminine energy and the lunar cycle. Its branches are flexible, expressing movement and change rather than resistance. It is a tree of enchantment and dreaming, enhancing a person's confidence in his or her intuition and the tree inspires leaps of imagination.

BEALTAINE

To the Celts, time was circular rather than linear. This is reflected in their commencing each day and each festival at dusk rather than dawn, a custom comparable to that of the Jewish Sabbath.

Bealtaine is celebrated around 1 May and is sacred to the god Belanus (the shining one). The word derives from '*Beltinne*' ('fires of Bel'). Bealtaine is a time of fertility when the cattle are set free from their winter quarters and driven between the cleansing fires. It is a time of feasting, fairs and the mating of livestock. Foods eaten at the Bealtaine feast may include honey products, mead, fruit, fish and milk products.

It has been suggested that the sacred fires of Bealtaine were actually a form of sympathetic magic that encouraged the sun to cast its warmth upon the earth.

Bealtaine and its opposite, Samhain, divide the year into two seasons, the dark winter and the bright summer. As Samhain honours the dead so Bealtaine, as its opposite, honours life. The sun reigns over the moon and now begins a time of magic and divination.

Bealtaine is the time when people get up at dawn and gather branches and flowers to decorate their homes. Leaves of the rowan along with primroses and buttercups were hung over the door and placed on the windowsills and the colour green would be worn to honour Mother Nature.

The sacred fire would be lit by the druids on the Hill of Uisneach. This had the power to heal and purify and its light would stretch out across the land for all to see. It celebrates the burning away of winter and the return of life to the earth. It was said that cinders and torches would transfer some of the sacred fire to every hearth in the land so that each and every person could share in its power.

There are many superstitions concerning this time and it is the one day of the year when you give nothing away. Even if a stranger called to a house looking for a light or a bit of butter, they would be turned away. Depending on which part of the country you were in, the customs were observed. In some parts on May Day, you should not dig, whitewash, bathe in the sea or take out a boat. At this time 'the gentry' (the fairies) were on the move and it was important not to upset them. It was also believed that on this day you could not venture out but if you had to go out for some reason then you were advised to carry a piece of iron in your pocket for protection against the gentry. If you had no iron then a sprig of rowan would do just as well. People would also leave a gift of food or drink for the fairies on the doorstep or under a hawthorn tree. The first water taken from the well at Bealtaine was known to be full of good luck and healing, but in the wrong hands it could be used to do harm to others. It was also a common belief that children born on the first day of May had the gift of second sight but unfortunately they were destined to die young. The 1 May was also the traditional day when tenants had to go up to the 'big house' to pay their rent to the landlord.

Weather-watching was an important pastime and the appearance of the sky and the moon, the strength and direction of the wind, and the amount of rainfall were all indications of the coming summer. If it was wet and windy, that was a good sign as it was an omen of good harvests to come. A cold, easterly wind was a bad sign and frost was an indicator of hard times ahead. Snow was such a bad omen that the farmers expected the landlord to forego the rent for the next half year (fat chance of that).

Family health was important on this day as it was believed that any injury sustained at this time would be very difficult to cure and may be a long time to heal. However, this was also considered the best time to gather medicinal herbs to replenish the medicine chest and it was said that the first butter made from the milk gathered on May Day would make a powerful ointment.

Bealtaine was a time of unabashed sexuality and promiscuity when marriages of a year and a day could be undertaken. In the distant past, young people would spend the entire night in the woods 'a-Maying' and then dance around the phallic maypole the next morning. Older married couples were allowed to remove their wedding rings (and the restrictions they imply) for this one night. There is absolutely no way you would get away with using that as an excuse today so if any of you are thinking about it, forget it.

LUGHNASADH

Lughnasadh is the beginning of the harvest season, also known as the 'Harvest of the First Fruits' (Anglo-Saxon), and the time of the funeral games of the Celtic goddess Tailtiu. Tailtiu died clearing a forest so that the land could be cultivated. As she lay on her death-bed, she spoke to those who had gathered around her. She asked that funeral games be instituted in her honour and that her foster son Lugh should lead the games.

Tailtiu prophesied that as long as the games were held, Ireland would be known for its song. Tailtiu gave her name to Teltown, County Meath, and it was there that the festival of Lughnasadh was traditionally held, eventually evolving into a huge tribal gathering. The high king presided over the legal agreements, disputes and polit-ical problems of the day. Athletes competed against each other, artists and entertainers showed off their talents, and traders gathered to sell their wares. Another important ritual that took place was that of 'handfasting' where couples would be joined together for a year and a day. If all went well then it would become a permanent arrangement and if not they would return the following year to separate.

Throughout the centuries we have celebrated the harvest and we still continue to do so. Lughnasadh has been given additional names over the years. Here in our corner of County Mayo, it is also known as 'Reek Sunday' or 'Garland Sunday' and people climb our local mountain, Croagh Patrick ('the Reek'). In some areas it is known as 'Bilberry Sunday'; again celebrations include climbing a local hill or mountain. Others call it Lammas (Anglo-Saxon).

In some parts of Ireland, the nearest Sunday to Lughnasadh was known as 'Cally Sunday'. It was the traditional day to lift the first new potatoes. The man of the house would dig the first stalk while the woman of the house would wear a new white apron and cook them, covering the kitchen floor with green rushes in their honour. The family would give thanks that the 'hungry month' of July was over and the harvest had begun. Initially the custom of first fruits usually applied to grain, but in later days, when grain crops were the province of large landowners, common people had no grain of their own to offer. The first fruits custom was therefore transferred to potatoes, an offering available to everyone with a patch of ground and widely grown as a subsistence crop.

'Cally' is a mixture of potato mashed together with butter, milk and sliced onion.

Lughnasadh was also a time when people would visit sacred or holy wells and leave offerings. By visiting the hilltops and the wells you were celebrating both the summit and the depths of the earth. Another name that is used for Lughnasadh gatherings is 'wake fairs' and is when a symbol of the god is placed in the field after harvest. The offering or symbol is usually in the shape of a corn dolly. The making of corn dollies is an ancient craft going back thousands of years. Before Christianity took hold in Ireland (and even afterwards), it was believed within the traditional pagan agricultural culture that the spirit of the corn lived amongst the crop and that when the crop was harvested it was effectively made homeless. The people believed that as they cut the harvest the spirit retreated before them. The last bunch of corn was therefore kept and given to the oldest man to plait and keep on the wall to house the spirit. When the following year's crop was sewn the spirit would be returned to the field by being shaken from last year's corn bunch. It was believed that this preserved the spirit at harvest time and ensured the success of next year's harvest. Ivy was a symbol of rebirth and so it wasn't uncommon to dress the corn dolly with a headdress of ivy and it has always been the tradition to plough the previous year's dolly back into the field the following year.

Traces of corn dolly shapes that date back to 2000 BC have been found.

SAMHAIN

As the wheel of the year turns, the days of autumn drawing closer, it brings with it the pagan feast of Samhain or the old Celtic New Year's Day. It was once considered the climax of the year's events, a time to light the sacred fire that would bring light to the dark days of winter. It was a time when we could converse with our ancestors, the veil between the two worlds was at its thinnest and the dead could once again walk among us.

There is more than one other world. There is what other cultures might call the fairy world, the magical lands of the Tuatha Dé Danaan who became known as the people of the sidhe, those who live in the Hollow Hills. There is also the other world proper, where we go when we die. Part of our spirit remains there, a trace of us, while the more integrated self is reborn. When we pray to the ancestors we access the sum of all the wisdom learned by all the people through all the long years. There is the homeland where the gods and goddesses dwell, where we can access the archetypes (such as the warrior, or the chief or the bard). All these worlds are open to you at Samhain, provided you seek them with a gentle heart and a respectful purpose.

The Celtic belief in an other world was very complex and very strong. As you died in this world you were reborn in that world. Death here was celebrated for the birth in the other world and birth here was marked with mourning for the death in the other world. There was a constant exchange of souls between the two. With such a belief you can see how a celebration of death at the moment of the New Year is very appropriate and how there was none of the fear and morbidity associated with death that has become so much a part of modern life.

Samhain, summer's end, marks one of the two great festivals of the Celtic year and it once divided the year into two seasons: the light and the dark, at Bealtaine on 1 May and Samhain on 1 November. In Scotland and Ireland, the festival is also known as *Oíche Shamhna*, while in Wales it is *Nos Galan Gaeaf*, the eve of the winter's calendar, or the first day of winter. Some believe that Samhain was the more important festival, marking the beginning of a whole new year, as the Celtic day began at night. It was the time of the dark silence when the seeds began to stir beneath the earth and the trees began to whisper to each other.

In the country year, Samhain was when the herders led the cattle and sheep down from their summer hillside pastures to the shelter of stable and byre. The hay that would feed them during the winter had to be stored in sturdy thatched ricks, tied down securely against storms. The livestock destined for the table were slaughtered, after being ritually devoted to the gods in pagan times. All the harvest must be gathered in – barley, oats, wheat, turnips and apples – and if the gods and goddesses had been kind to you, then your larder would be full. With the advent of November came the *gaoithe sidhe*, the fairy wind, and now the fairies would blast every growing plant with their breath, blighting any nuts and berries remaining on the hedgerows. Peat and wood for winter fires were stacked high by the hearth. It was a joyous time of family reunion, when all members of the household worked together baking, salting meat, smoking hams and making preserves for the winter feasts to come. The endless days of summer gave way to a warm, dim and often smoky room; the sounds of summer were replaced by the chatter of voices, young and old, human and animal, and the smell of candle wax or the glow of a turf fire. It was a time to sit around the hearth and listen to the stories of old.

In early Ireland, people gathered at the ritual centres of the tribes, for Samhain was the principal calendar feast of the year. The greatest assembly was the 'Feast of Tara', focusing on the royal seat of the high king as the heart of the sacred land, the point of conception for the New Year. In every household throughout the country, hearth fires were extinguished. Everyone waited for the druids to light the new fire of the year, not at Tara, but at Tlachtga, a hill twelve miles to the north-west. It marked the burial place of Tlachtga, daughter of the great druid Mogh Ruith, who may once have been a goddess in her own right in a former age.

At all the turning points of the Celtic year, the gods drew near to earth. At Samhain, many sacrifices and gifts were offered up in thanksgiving for the harvest. Personal offerings in the form of objects symbolising the wishes of the giver or ailments to be healed were thrown into the sacred fire and at the end of the cer-emonies, brands were lit from the great fire of Tara to re-kindle all the home fires of the tribe, as at Bealtaine. As they received the flame that marked this time of beginnings, people surely felt a sense of the kindling of new dreams, projects and hopes for the year to come.

People generally celebrate Samhain on 31 October though there is also the tradition that has become widely known as Old Samhain. This is celebrated mainly on 8 November, although (rarely) it is also celebrated on 7 November here as this is closer to the original date of Samhain in the pre-Gregorian calendar and almost all traditional druids and witches in Celtic areas mark this day in some way or another.

Christian Influence over Samhain
The once spiritual event of Samhain has now become one of the most commercialised festivals in modern times. It has been pol-luted and corrupted by both the recognised religions and corporate institutions.

As Christianity spread throughout the Celtic regions, an attempt was made to remove the pagan influences of their festivals and replace them instead with a Christian-sanctioned one. Many pagan festivals were adapted – Oestara became Easter and Yule evolved into Christmas. Pope Boniface IV renamed Samhain, which fell on 1 November, as Hallowmas or All Saints' Day, intended as a day to honour dead saints. 2 November became All Souls' Day, when prayers were to be offered to the souls of all who the departed and those who were waiting in purgatory for entry into heaven. The last day of October began to be called All Hallows' Eve and this eventually evolved into 'Halloween'.

This Christian celebration of the day of the dead has many similarities to Samhain rituals, such as the wearing of masks, parades of ghosts and skeletons, and special food offerings to the dead. However, Halloween not only hijacked the beliefs and practices of our ancestors, it insults the very culture it was stolen from. Not content with mocking the ancient rituals, such as divination and laying a place at the table for the visiting ancestor, mainstream Churches would have people believe that its origins lie in devil worship, which is a little annoying when you consider that the pagans did not believe in the devil. However, it certainly tells us more about the orthodox religions than our pagan past.

Many Samhain rituals, traditions and customs have been passed down throughout the centuries and are still practised in various countries on Halloween today. As a feast of divination, this was the night for peering into the future. There are many types of divination that are traditional to Halloween so it's only possible to mention a few of them here. Girls were told to place hazelnuts along the front of the fire grate, each one symbolising one of her suitors. She could then divine her future husband by chanting, 'If you love me, pop and fly; if you hate me, burn and die'.

Several methods used the apple, a popular Halloween fruit and long believed to be a sacred fruit due to the pentacle within. You should slice an apple into two halves (to reveal the five-pointed star/pentacle) and eat it by candlelight before a mirror. Your future spouse will then appear over your shoulder. Alternatively, peel an apple, making sure the peel comes off in one long strand, reciting the following:

> I pare this apple round and round again. My sweetheart's name
> to flourish on the plain. I fling the unbroken paring o'er my head.
> My sweetheart's letter on the ground to read.

Or you might set a snail to crawl through the ashes of your hearth. The considerate little creature will then spell out the initial letter of your intended as it moves.

Bobbing for apples was actually a custom the Celts inherited from the Romans when conquered by the Roman Empire. Romans honoured the harvest god, Pomona, and because the apple was a venerated fruit, many rituals revolved around it. The Celts simply incorporated bobbing for apples into Samhain tradition.

Another possibility is that bobbing for apples could represent the remnants of a pagan 'baptism' rite called a *seining*, according to some writers. The water-filled tub is a latter-day cauldron of regeneration into which the novice's head is immersed. The fact that the participant in this folk game was usually blindfolded with hands tied behind the back also puts one in mind of a traditional craft initiation ceremony.

Bobbing for apples was also a game of divination. Single girls looking for a mate would carve their initials onto an apple before putting it into a bucket of water. Young men would take it in turns to 'bob' for an apple. The one they chose would have the initials of their intended carved upon it.

Carving jack-o'-lanterns was a custom practised by Irish children during Samhain. Using a potato or turnip, they would carve out an image and place a candle inside to pay tribute to Jack, an Irish villain so amoral that he was rejected by both God and the Devil. Legend has it that Jack wandered the world, looking for a place to rest, finding it only in a carved-out vegetable. Later when the Irish emigrated to America, pumpkins were used instead.

Some traditions say that the carved-out pumpkin originated from a Celtic practice of putting an antecedent's skull outside of their home during Samhain. Others say that the jack-o'-lantern was used to ward off evil spirits which were brought forth on All Hallows' Eve.

Halloween masks and costumes originated from the Celtic belief that on Samhain, while restless and often evil spirits crossed the thin void from the spirit world, a mask would make the wearer unrecognisable from these ghosts. Druidic rites also involved the wearing of masks, often made of animals' skins, as the wearers told fortunes and practised other divination rituals.

Here is one story we tell in Mayo when we're sitting around the fire at Samhain/Halloween.

Jack-o'-Lantern

According to Irish folklore, a man named Jack, well known for his drunkenness and quick temper, got very drunk at a local pub on Halloween. As his life began to slip away, the Devil appeared to claim Jack's soul. Jack, eager to stay alive, begged the Devil to let him have just one more drink before he died. The Devil agreed; however, Jack was short of money and so he asked the Devil if he wouldn't mind assuming the shape of a sixpence so he could pay for the drink, saying that after the transaction the Devil could change back. Now, the Devil is quite gullible in almost all of these folk tales, so you won't be surprised when I tell you that he agreed once again and changed himself into a six-pence. Jack immediately grabbed the coin and shoved it into his wallet, which just happened to have a cross-shaped catch on it. The Devil, now imprisoned in the wallet, screamed with rage and ordered Jack to release him. Jack agreed to free the Devil from his wallet if the Devil agreed not to bother Jack for a whole year. Again, the Devil agreed to Jack's terms. Realising he now had a new lease on life, at least for a year, Jack decided to mend his ways. For a time Jack was good to his wife and children and began to attend church and give to charity but eventually he slipped back into his evil ways.

The next Halloween, as Jack was heading home, the Devil appeared and demanded that Jack accompany him. Once again Jack, not too eager to die, distracted the Devil by pointing to a nearby apple tree. Jack convinced the Devil to get him an apple out of the tree and even offered to hoist the Devil up on his shoulders to help him get the apple. The Devil, fooled once again by Jack, climbed into the tree and plucked an apple. Jack took out a knife and carved a cross into the trunk of the tree. Trapped once again, the Devil howled to be released and told Jack he would give him ten years of peace in exchange for his release. Jack, on the other hand, insisted the Devil never bother him again. The Devil agreed and was released.

Almost a year later Jack's body, unable to withstand his evil ways, gave out and Jack died. When Jack tried to enter heaven, he was told that he would not be allowed in because of his meanness. When Jack attempted to gain entry into hell, the Devil, still smarting from years of humiliation, refused Jack admission. However, being the kind Devil that he was, he threw Jack a piece of coal to help him find his way in the dark of limbo. Jack put the piece of coal into a turnip and it became known as a jack-o'-lantern. On Halloween, if you look you can still see Jack's flame burning dimly as he searches for a home. Of course, when Irish people went to America they discovered the pumpkin, which soon replaced the turnip as it was easier to carve.

THE ROCK OF BOHEA

In 1987 a local historian discovered that while standing at the Rock of Bohea (not far from the town of Westport, which is about 7km, or just over 4 miles, from Croagh Patrick), the setting sun, rather than disappearing behind Croagh Patrick, actually rolls down the north slope of the mountain. This phenomenon lasts about twenty minutes and occurs on the 18 April and 24 August each year. These two dates, along with 21 December, split the year into three equal parts and it is thought that they were used to celebrate sowing and harvesting seasons as well as being a time for handfasting.

One can only imagine the effect that the spectacle of the rolling sun would have had on the primitive people as they witnessed their druids commanding the sun god Lugh to appear. The rock is covered in cup and ring marks and is one of the finest examples of Neolithic rock art in Europe. With the coming of Christianity, the Rock of Bohea was used by clergy as a mass rock during times of conflict between the Catholic and Protestant Church when Catholic priest's had to conduct the mass in secret and it was given the name St Patrick's Chair.

Close to the Rock of Bohea, there is a small untended wood in which there is a *cillín,* an unconsecrated place of burial for unbaptised children and others that the Church deemed unfit to be buried in consecrated ground.

ANNAGH-KILLADANGAN

Less than a kilometre from Croagh Patrick, near the town of Louisburgh, is the ancient ritual site of Annagh-Killadangan, which has a row of standing stones at its centre. This stone row aligns with the setting sun at 8.40 p.m. on 21 December each year. The sun sets into a notch on the east ridge of Croagh Patrick and so, on the same day as the rising sun is celebrated at Newgrange, the setting sun retires to its sacred celestial home at Croagh Patrick.

Up until AD 1113, Lent or St Patrick's Day (17 March) was the accepted time of year to make a pilgrimage to Croagh Patrick, but in AD 1113 a thunderbolt is said to have killed thirty of the pilgrims, which resulted in the pilgrimage period being changed to summer, the most popular dates being the last Friday or Sunday of July. This story can be seen as an example of the old pagan gods gaining revenge on their Christian usurpers.

Although Croagh Patrick was originally a pagan sanctuary for the celebration of life's abundance, under Christianity it became the scene of penance for supposed sinfulness. Many of the Christian pilgrims ascended the mountain barefoot, or even on their knees, as an act of atonement.

HONEYMOON: AN IRISH TRADITION

The term 'honeymoon' is packed with symbolism. Mead, or honey wine, is sweet and symbolises the particular sweetness of the first month of marriage. It is a time free from the stresses and tensions put on the relationship by everyday life. The moon symbolises the phases or cycles of the couple's relationship as it waxes and wanes from full moon to full moon. Like the moon, the couple's relationship can be expected to have its brighter moments and its darker ones. Being tied in with the moon's cycle, the one-month period of time was associated with the woman's menstrual cycle and thus fertility.

The term 'honeymoon' did not evolve from a term of endearment or the description of an event. It literally depicted a period of time during which a particular marital convention was followed, specifically what the bride and groom did for one full moon after their wedding. Were it not for some Irish monks in the Middle Ages, who originally produced mead (honey wine) for medicinal purposes, none of us would refer to the post-matrimonial period as a 'honeymoon'.

Ever since the fame of the monks' brew spread throughout medieval Ireland, it has become essential to toast the bride and groom after the wedding before waving them off on their life together. It was used both as a final toast and a proper beginning of the marriage. Following the wedding, the bride and groom were provided with enough mead to toast each other after their wedding, hence the term 'honeymoon'.

This delicate yet potent drink was not only considered the best way to start a new marriage, it was also believed to enhance such valued qualities as fertility and virility. On numerous occasions the groom, laced with generous amounts of mead, was carried by his friends to the bedside of his bride. If nine months later a bouncing baby appeared, credit was given to the mead – and they say romance is dead.

Mead's influence was so great that the halls of Tara, where the high kings of Ireland ruled, were called the House of the Mead Circle. In Celtic mythology, a river of mead flows through paradise.

It became the chief drink of the Irish and was often referred to in Gaelic poetry. Its fame quickly spread and soon a medieval banquet was not complete without it.

Stories making reference to mead have been found as early as the fifth century and it was in wide use by the Middle Ages. So it seems that the 'honeymoon' tradition may be even older than our contemporary wedding.

Good health and a long life to you.

Dea-shláinte agus saol fada chugat.

BIBLIOGRAPHY

BOOKS

Chambers, Anne, *Granuaile: Grace O'Malley – Ireland's Pirate Queen, c. 1530-1603* (Dublin: Gill and MacMillan, 2009).

Henry, Sean, *Tales from the West of Ireland* (Dublin: Mercier Press, 1980).

Hyde, Douglas, *The Stone of Truth, and Other Irish Folktales* (Indiana: Rowman & Littlefield Publishers, 1979).

Jocelyn, Robert, *Progress of the Reformation in Ireland – Extracts from a series of letters written from the West of Ireland to a friend in England, in September 1851* (London: James Nisbet, 1851).

Nolan, Rita, *Within the Mullet* (Ballina, Ireland: Western People Printing, 1997).

Otway, Caesar, *Sketches in Erris and Tyrawly* (Dublin: William Curry, 1841).

Scott, Michael, *Irish Animal Tales* (Cork: Mercier Press, 1989).

White, T.H., *The Godstone and the Blackymor* (London: Jonathan Cape/Random House, 1959).

Wright, T. (ed.), *The Historical Works of Giraldus Cambrensis* (London: George Bell & Sons, 1913).

Yeats, W.B., *The Land of Heart's Desire* (Ithaca, New York: Cornell University Press, 2002).

Websites

http://irishislands.info/inishkea.html, accessed 9 November 2013.
http://multitext.ucc.ie/d/Famine, accessed 10 February 2014.
Irish famine, page 16 (*fear gorta*).
www.turtlebunbury.com/history/history_irish/history_irish_bigwind.htm, accessed 2 December 2013
www.gutenberg.org/files/1241/1241-h/1241-h.htm Synge, J.M., *Well of the Saints*, accessed 18 January 2014.

Archives

The Irish Tourist Association Topographical and General Survey in 1945, Kibeagh Parish Archives, 'The Ghost of Barnalyra Wood', page 10.
Dublin Penny Journal, vol. 1, no. 18, 27 October 1832. 'The Remarkable Seal of Clew Bay'.
South Mayo Family Research Journal, published in 1995. 'The Night of the Big Wind'.
Journal of the North Mayo Historical Society, 1982, Gertrude O'Reilly McHale, 'The Story of Barney Moran'.

If you enjoyed this book, you may also be interested in…

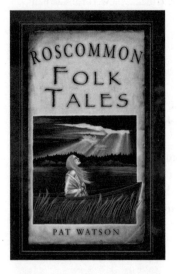

Roscommon Folk Tales

PAT WATSON

Roscommon has as many stories as there are people travelling its roads, passed down from generation to generation, and a wealth of them are gathered together here in this unique volume. Included here are intriguing stories of a vanishing lake, Oileán na Sioga (The Fairy Island), and the miracles of St Kieran, along with darker tales of the battles of Queen Méabh, the Monster of Lough Ree, and the story of Betty of Roscommon, Ireland's first (and only) hang woman – not to mention the fantastical accounts of encounters with leprechauns, pookas, giants and banshees.

978 1 84588 784 1

Galway Bay Folk Tales

RAB FULTON

From the saints of the Dark Ages to modern-day sinners, Galway Bay is the source of some of Ireland's most magical tales. In this book local storyteller Rab Fulton takes the reader through Galway's past, recalling the myths and legends that shaped the area's history – from the quarrelsome giants who in their rage created the Aran Isles, to the corpse that flew through the air at the very first Galway Arts Festival. Also featuring tales of magic swans, ferocious queens, a city beneath the waves and a gruesome case of accidental cannibalism.

978 1 84588 779 7

Visit our website and discover thousands of other History Press books.

www.thehistorypress.ie